APOCALYPSE
FOR
BEGINNERS

APOCALYPSE

FOR

BEGINNERS

NICOLAS DICKNER

TRANSLATED BY LAZER LEDERHENDLER

Portobello
BOOKS

First published by Portobello Books 2011
This paperback edition published 2011

Portobello Books
12 Addison Avenue
London
W11 4QR

A CIP catalogue record is available from the British Library

9 8 7 6 5 4 3 2 1

ISBN 978 1 84627 260 8

www.portobellobooks.com

Mixed Sources
Product group from well-managed
forests and other controlled sources
www.fsc.org Cert no. TF-COC-002227
© 1996 Forest Stewardship Council
FSC

Printed and bound in Great Britain by CPI Bookmarque, Croydon

For Z and G

N.D.

—

For David, my son

L.L.

"The future ain't what it used to be."

YOGI BERRA

I. VAPORIZED

August 1989. Ronald Reagan had vacated the White House, the Cold War was winding down and the outdoor municipal swimming pool was, once again, closed for maintenance.

Rivière-du-Loup was immersed in a chicken broth of pollen-saturated, yellowish air, and I wandered glumly around the neighbourhood, my towel around my neck. Just three days remained before the start of the new school year, and nothing but a few good laps through chlorinated water could have boosted my morale.

I ended up at the municipal stadium. Not a soul in sight. The lines on the baseball field were freshly drawn and the scent of chalk still wafted around. I'd never cared about baseball but, for no particular reason, I loved stadiums. I walked past the dugout. On an old sun-bleached newspaper a column of tanks at Tiananmen Square could just barely be made out.

That was when I noticed the girl sitting up in the very last row. Her nose was buried in a book, as though she was killing time waiting for the next game to begin.

Without giving it too much thought, I climbed up the bleachers in her direction.

I'd never seen her in the neighbourhood. She was thin, with bony hands and a face studded with freckles. The visor of her Mets cap was pulled down low over her eyes and the left knee of her jeans was ripped. The jeans were not of the trendy acid-washed variety, but rough-cut work pants, an ancient pair of Levi's salvaged from some coal mine in the New Mexico desert.

Her back pressed against the guardrail, she was reading a language-learning manual: *Teach Yourself Russian at Home, Volume 13*.

I sat down without speaking. She made no sign of noticing me.

The wooden benches scorched our behinds. The sun poured down so mercilessly I was tempted to turn my towel into a turban, but I was afraid of appearing ridiculous. High overhead I could see a 747 tracing long parallel lines of cirrus clouds in the sky. Dry weather ahead.

I was on the verge of spouting some meteorological small talk when the girl tilted up the visor of her cap.

"Last night I dreamt about the bomb at Hiroshima."

A few seconds went by while I pondered this unconventional preamble.

"Why specifically the Hiroshima bomb?"

She folded her arms.

"The destructive power of modern bombs is unimaginable. Take, for example, an ordinary ballistic missile, about five hundred kilotons. The explosion is enough to send a chunk of tectonic plate into orbit. It's beyond what the human brain can grasp."

Where was this girl from? I couldn't pin down her accent. English? Acadian? My guess was Brayon—from Edmundston, New Brunswick, to be exact. She yanked an empty Cracker Jack box out from between two planks and proceeded to turn it into confetti.

"Little Boy had a yield of approximately fifteen kilotons. Not exactly a firecracker, but easier to measure all the same. If it exploded over our heads, at six hundred metres— the same altitude as the Hiroshima explosion—the shock wave would flatten the city over a radius of 1.5 kilometres. That amounts to an area of seven square kilometres. Which represents . . ."

She squinted, concentrating on the massive mental calculation.

"Two thousand five hundred baseball fields."

She stopped shredding the Cracker Jack box long enough for her arms to sweep instructively over the landscape.

"The shopping mall would be pulverized, bungalows would be blown to pieces, cars would be sent flying like cardboard boxes, the lampposts would flop down on the ground. And that's just the shock wave. Then there would be the thermal radiation. Everything would be reduced to ash over dozens of square kilometres—way, way more baseball fields! Near the bomb, the heat would be greater than the temperature at the surface of the sun. Metal would liquefy. Sand would turn into little glass beads."

Having finished the shredding job, she weighed the pile of confetti in the palm of her hand.

"And do you know what would happen to *us*, two tiny, little primates made up of 60 per cent water?"

She gently turned her hand upside down and let the breeze carry the confetti off toward left field.

"We would be vaporized in three thousandths of a second."

She finally turned my way and took a good look at me, probably to gauge how well I'd held up to her lesson. Pretty well, by and large. Her gaze told me I had passed the test.

Her face softened, and I detected the hint of a friendly smile. Then, without saying another word, she plunged back into her Russian handbook.

The shock wave having left me slightly worse for wear, I dropped back against the guardrail. I observed the girl sideways as I wiped my forehead with a corner of the towel. I could have sworn she generated a magnetic field—the radiation of her 195 IQ.

Not only had I never seen this girl before, but I had never seen any girl like her. And just as I was thinking this, it dawned on me that if I ever had to be vaporized in the company of someone else, I would definitely want it to be her.

2. THE PET SHOP

Her name was Hope Randall and she had just rolled in from Yarmouth, Nova Scotia.

"Do you know where that is?"

She outlined a map of Nova Scotia in the air with her index finger, and stabbed a pinhole at the southern tip of the peninsula, opposite Maine. A distance of 1200 kilometres from Rivière-du-Loup.

"Never heard of it."

"Doesn't matter."

Hope and her mother had arrived in town three days earlier and moved into a house on Amyot Street that was wedged between the Clean-O-Matic launderette and the kitchen of the Chinese Garden Restaurant. Two high temples of local cleanliness.

She turned the key a few times in the lock and gave the door a kick.

"Welcome to the Randall Pet Shop!"

Suddenly it came back to me. A pet shop had been located there—L'Arche de Nowé (sic)—but it had closed down the previous winter and been converted into a (moderately) acceptable apartment. The position of the counter, the shelves and the aquariums could still be deduced from outlines on the floor. An all-pervading aroma of Asian stir-fries hung in the air but it could not disguise the lingering odours of parrot droppings, chinchilla piss and dry cat food.

The furniture (included in the rent) consisted of a rickety table, four chairs, a set of dented appliances and a couch that, with no TV in sight, was the epitome of pointlessness.

Hope assured me that they been there for less than seventy-two hours, yet every corner of the place was piled high with an inordinate supply of food: sacks of flour, bags of ramen, containers full of water or cooking oil, canned food of every description. In fact, the only non-edible item was a small stack of *Teach Yourself Russian at Home* (volumes 8, 14 and 17), to which Hope now delicately added the volume she had been reading at the municipal stadium.

"Thirsty?"

I nodded. While she poured me a glass of water I scanned the pet shop looking for adjoining rooms. There were none, except for an oddly spacious bathroom—no doubt the former Lizards' Lair. But where did they sleep? Hope second-guessed me and pointed to the couch.

"It folds out. I sleep in the bathtub, with the door shut. It's impossible to get any sleep within ten feet of my mother."

"She snores?"

"No. She talks in her sleep."

"Really?"

I took a sip of water. It tasted suspiciously metallic.

"So, what does she say?"

Hope seemed annoyed by the question and began to chew at her thumbnail.

"No idea. Stuff in Assyrian."

"Assyrian?"

"Assyrian or Aramaic—who knows? I have no clue about dead languages."

She chewed off a sliver of fingernail and spat it out.

"People in my family are polyglots."

"I can see that," I said, pointing my foot at the Russian handbooks.

"I also started to learn German, but I had to abandon my books in Yarmouth. They wouldn't fit in the car."

"Abandon?"

"Yes. We left in the middle of the night because . . ."

She sighed.

"Okay. I might as well start at the beginning."

Mary Hope Juliet Randall, called Hope, was the youngest member of a family that, for an indeterminate number of generations—some put the number at seven—had been afflicted by a serious obsession with the end of the world.

The Randins, a family with vaguely Acadian roots, had been deported by the British in 1755. They landed in Maryland, adopted the name Randall—though without giving in to assimilation—and eventually returned to Nova Scotia, where they spent the ensuing decades squatting barren patches of peat bog.

In fact, the family obsession with the apocalypse might reasonably be traced back to that geopolitical trauma. Indeed, wouldn't it be expected, or even inevitable, for a line of exiled farmers to be somewhat sensitive about urban sprawl, major disasters and the natural course of history? Yet there was no consensus around this theory, and certain genealogists favoured the hypothesis of a congenital condition due to inbreeding (the Randalls were confirmed homebodies).

One thing, however, was certain: the same symptoms recurred with choreographic precision from one generation to the next. So, at puberty, every Randall was supernaturally made privy to the details of the end of the world—the date, the time, the exact form it would take.

As a rule, the vision came at night. Actually, it wasn't exactly a vision, which could have been dismissed as a mere nightmare. No. The Randalls tuned in to the apocalypse on a visceral level. They felt the patter of rain and the burn of shrapnel on their skin, they suffocated in the fires, tasted the ash, heard the screams, smelled the stink of rotting corpses.

The Randalls called this phenomenon the "Night-time Revelation," the "Light," the "Prediction," or, more often than not, the "Spell from Hell."

Every Randall was apprised of a different date, which in no way made it easier for them to be taken seriously. What's more, a Randall who outlived his or her end of the world would then experience a mental breakdown and an inclination to damage public property. The story would usually end in an asylum or suchlike.

Indeed, the Randall family tree could be used in a course on the history of psychiatry in North America over the past one hundred and fifty years, from the cold shower to the lobotomy, occupational therapy, the straitjacket and lithium, right through to deinstitutionalization.

Case No. 1: Harry Randall Truman, the patriarch, lost his mind in the fall of 1835, shortly after the passage of Halley's comet. He prophesied the return of Moses aboard an incandescent whaler, and subsequently burned down the barn of the Presbyterian pastor. The neighbours wrestled him to the ground, tied him up and shipped him off to the Halifax Mental Asylum, where he lived out his days in the wing reserved for pyromaniacs and other sociopaths.

Case No. 37: Gary Randall holed up for fifteen years in a plywood shack that boasted a window through which he would greet any psychotherapist (a rare bird) with a few volleys of his 12-gauge shotgun. They found him clutching his firearm one morning after the temperature had dropped to 40 below—stiff, blue and completely divested of his obsession.

Case No. 53: Henry Randall Jr., Hope's grandfather and a veteran of the Depression, behaved more constructively. He channelled his anxiety into founding the Minoritarian Reform Church of the Seventh Ruminant, a para-Christian sect that predicted Armageddon would take place on June 12, 1977. As good a way as any to kill time. The church existed until the aforementioned date, after which Henry killed himself by gulping down a fistful of roofing nails.

And so it went with Gary Randall, Harry Randall, Harriet Randall, Hanna Randall, Henry Randall, Randolph Randall, Handy Randall, Hans Randall, Hank Randall, Annabel Thibodeau (née Randall), Henryette Leblanc Randall, Hattie Randall, Pattie Randall and so on, while the planet persisted in spinning around like a bad joke.

Ann Randall was born in Yarmouth in March 1954, on the same day that the Americans tested a new hydrogen bomb in the Marshall Islands.

She was a quiet young girl, stunningly and precociously beautiful, whose gift for languages was phenomenal. At the age of ten she had a full command of English and French and was learning Latin from an old Vulgate stolen from the church sacristy, an autodidactic theft to which the priest turned a blind eye.

Her lonely childhood was spent between a father kept busy presiding over the Minoritarian Reform Church of the Seventh Ruminant, and a disturbed mother, whom Ann lost when she was twelve years old. That summer the poor woman, exhausted from waiting for a firestorm that never materialized, swallowed the entire contents of the family medicine cabinet: pills, cough syrup and bandages. After her stomach had been pumped, she was sent to Halifax for emergency psychiatric treatment—and never came back.

On September 1, 1966, at dawn, after two days of cramps and migraines, Ann Randall, still shaken by her mother's confinement, woke up sweating so profusely that the sheets clung to her body. Off Yarmouth, the rumbling of a storm could be heard.

From that moment Ann knew—and would never for an instant forget—that the end of the world would take place in the summer of 1989.

She was struck at once by the vision's lack of detail. The summer of 1989? That was all? Yet her cousins had assured her that not only would she be informed of the exact date of the end of the world (down to the minute) but that she would be presented with explicit images, tactile sensations, smells. She had been promised a revelation in CinemaScope, but all she received was a blurred and poorly framed slide.

Sitting up in her bed, she became aware of another event—one that was wet, sticky and unmistakable. She slid three fingers between her thighs and they came back stained with brownish blood. Her Spell from Hell was sealed.

Ann went to school for another few years, earning consistently high marks, but she dropped out in Grade 12 without giving any reason. And actually, no one asked. She took a job at the municipal library (comprising a few bookcases in the basement of the town hall), where she shelved books and polished her Latin.

When she was eighteen Ann had a fleeting affair with a court clerk and became pregnant. It was, of course, an accident; procreation among the Randalls was always purely accidental. The circumstances of this particular nocturnal episode remained hazy, but according to local legend, the *act* was committed after closing time in the children's book aisle. The gossip was that Ann had been looking for trouble.

The clerk, a family man and an upright citizen, stayed out of sight and left Ann to deal on her own with public opinion and the tiny carbon copy of his genetic code.

The pregnancy set an entire series of fuses popping in Ann Randall's brain, which was immediately subjected to waves of apocalyptic anxiety and uncontrollable manias. For example, she earmarked half of the library's annual budget for the purchase of an extravagant collection of ancient texts: bibles in Aramaic, Hebrew and Greek, a facsimile of the Dead Sea Scrolls, the Epic of Gilgamesh, the Enûma Eliš and the Book of the Dead. She never bothered going home any more, instead spending her nights in the town hall basement studying the dead languages of Mesopotamia and eating ramen noodles.

After several months, completely worn out, she tried to end it all by swallowing a bottle of Aspirin, which resulted in severe liver damage. The examination at the hospital brought to light, first, the drug poisoning, then the psychotic episodes, and, finally, the existence of the fetus. Three diagnoses for the price of one.

She was referred to an obstetrician, who sent her on to a social worker, who entrusted her to a psychologist, who in turn transferred her to a psychiatrist, so that she eventually went home with a hefty prescription of 250 mg of clozapine, to be taken every morning with orange juice, along with a tablet of doxylamine for nausea.

Now that the psychotic episodes had stopped, Ann could resume her tasks at the library. Everything appeared to be under control. She floated in a state of euphoria, swelling at the midriff, shelving books, stamping cards. It was through this veil of medication that Hope came into the world, three weeks early (punctuality was undeniably on the wane for the Randalls).

Grandfather Henry came to the nursery, answering the call for help and stayed just long enough to take a quick look at the baby and declare that her name would be Mary Hope Juliet.

Mary Hope Juliet—airdropped into a cuckoo's nest.

5. A DISTURBING LOGIC

As an infant, Hope was perceptive and independent-minded. She rarely cried and refused the breast very early on. She had not inherited her mother's fragile beauty, but there was an undeniable gracefulness in her figure and her gestures. Her hair was straight and unruly, and the freckles that blossomed on her face during the heat wave of 1977 rounded out the impression of a little girl who had been abandoned in the heart of the Amazonian jungle.

The years went by. Ann shelved books and followed her prescribed dosage. Hope attended the elementary school across the street. She had few friends, and family visits were rare. The Randalls gathered at the funeral parlour every two months or so, each time an aunt or a cousin succumbed to her or his personal apocalypse, and such evenings were just about the only social life they had.

All in all, it was a life that held no surprises.

Things began to fall apart the day that Ann quit her job at the library, taking with her the collection of bibles (whose removal, as it happened, went quite unnoticed). She found a job as a cashier at Sobeys, and set about hoarding considerable quantities of food—enough to keep a large family self-sufficient for many months.

This food-related disorder was governed by a disturbing logic: Ann refused to buy fresh fruit and vegetables, that is, food whose value was necessarily ephemeral. She thought in terms of calories per cubic metre, protein and nutritional benefit. Above all, no perishables. She came home from Sobeys with enormous provisions: five-pound bags of rice, ten-pound sacks of potatoes, four cans each of red beans and stewed tomatoes, twenty cans each of tuna in oil, pears, peaches, peas. And ramen—hundreds of packets of ramen that she stored in every available space.

When her daughter asked her what the purpose was of all these supplies, Ann Randall answered mysteriously, "To barter, when the Chinese show up."

Hope was only eight and a half but already found her mother's sense of humour suspect.

6. *TEACH YOURSELF RUSSIAN AT HOME*

After a few relatively uneventful years, Social Services reactivated the Ann Randall file. A routine visit had made clear that something about this family was not quite right. Specifically, aside from the legal guardian's psychiatric history, here she was, storing packets of ramen and tins of sardines by the thousands. Suspicious.

Fortunately, Hope was on the alert. Whenever a social worker threatened to drop in on them, Hope would scrub the floor, pour a litre of bleach into the toilet bowl and fill a pretty wicker basket with apples and oranges. In this carefully prepared environment, Ann Randall managed to look almost ordinary.

The stratagem was repeated every six months, and Hope gradually learned to create an illusion of normalcy. She soon grasped that certain details appeared fishy, especially their not owning a television, which served not merely as another home appliance but as proof of one's allegiance to society. So Hope went out scavenging and came back with someone's discarded old black-and-white Zenith. The bottom part of the screen was dead, but as long as the set stayed turned off it did the trick.

As soon as the TV was installed in the dining room, the social workers' attitude shifted. They took note of this positive sign and their visits became less frequent. Between inspections, however, the television had to be stowed away. Ann Randall would not tolerate an apparatus that caused retinal cancer and rotted the brain.

The arrival of the television represented a turning point in Hope's life. Until then, the only source of information available in the house had been her mother's bible collection. Hope had read the King James version once, without skipping a single page, and that was enough, thank you very much.

Now, however, she locked herself in the closet every night to watch the international news on CBC, old late-night feature films, and, above all—that inviolable appointment—David Suzuki and *The Nature of Things*. Astronomy, genetics, chemistry: there was nothing that did not interest her. Every Friday night the good news emanating from Vancouver, British Columbia, was relayed from repeater to repeater across the continent via the Hertzian highway and touched down in a beat-up television inside a closet in Yarmouth, Nova Scotia, where it irradiated the brain of a young girl with a craving for science.

The Cold War was drawing to a close. The advent of Mikhail Gorbachev was a good omen, perestroika was a good omen and glasnost was a very, very good omen. From now on, there would be no more talk of nuclear holocaust; instead, speculation focused on the imminent opening of a McDonald's on Red Square.

Hope had the foresight to make collect calls to every Halifax bookstore with the aim of locating a Russian-language textbook. She finally tracked one down at the Book Room. The following week, a highly disgruntled postman delivered three enormous packages, tightly wrapped in brown paper, containing the seventeen volumes of *Teach Yourself Russian at Home*.

While her mother chewed on her nails in the kitchen, Hope shut herself in the closet, furtively turned on the TV, and in the stroboscopic glow of the screen learned all about personal pronouns, conjunctions and conjugations.

She was in the midst of memorizing her first irregular verbs when the Chernobyl accident occurred.

A simple maintenance oversight, a mere thirty seconds of negligence, and a nuclear power plant in the middle of the Ukraine began to melt down as easily as caramel on the stovetop. Hope stayed glued to the TV for three days. For the first time, the whole world could follow every moment of a calamity unfolding on Soviet soil, a scenario that two or three years earlier would have been the stuff of science fiction.

For Ann Randall, on the other hand, Chernobyl was one of several omens—there were, after all, only three years left before 1989—and she once again was stricken with a blend of anxiety and insomnia as well as abrupt and inexplicable bouts of feverish excitement. And there was something new: she began to speak Assyrian in her sleep.

Assyrian or Hebrew or possibly Sumerian, was what Hope surmised, on grounds that were actually rather thin. Her mother fell asleep each night reading a bulky multi-language bible. Was some sort of contamination taking place? At any rate, whatever it was bore no resemblance to Russian.

For Hope, self-appointed guardian of domestic balance, this apocalyptic psychosis was not some quaint family idiosyncrasy but a bona fide problem. So she dragged her progenitor to the psychiatrist, who confirmed that the dosage of clozapine, after many years of effectiveness, seemed no longer to be working. A new dosage and a new routine were prescribed.

What accounted for this sudden lack of response to the medication? The doctor could not say for sure. He raised various possibilities: the natural history of the illness, changes in the body's metabolism, the effects of habituation.

For her part, Hope believed there might be an undocumented incompatibility between clozapine and the international news.

Still, whatever the explanation, from now on she would have to intensify her efforts to preserve domestic stability. The resulting tension only heightened her solitary tendencies and increased the number of hours per week spent in her closet retreat.

She felt overwhelmed by the situation, but to whom could she turn for help? Certainly not the Randalls. They tolerated but did not really accept her, quite simply because Hope had not yet endured her Spell from Hell. What kind of Randall were you if you had no idea of your date for the end of the world? Barely a sub-Randall, a maggot, a foreign object orbiting around the family tree.

Hope walked the line between two worlds, unable to set her foot down in one or the other. Luckily she had David Suzuki.

7. STRUCK DOWN BY FATE

Inevitably, the summer of 1989 arrived.

Hope's mother was in the grip of indescribable dread, magnified because she did not exactly know what to expect. It had been some time since she had swallowed any pills whatsoever, and the unopened bottles of clozapine were gathering dust in the medicine cabinet. Consequently, she spent her evenings playing solitaire on the kitchen table and jumping at the slightest squeak, which her imagination immediately amplified and transformed into a cataclysm.

At all times the neighbour's television could be heard through the wall—a mixture of *The Price Is Right*, *Three's Company* and *Wok With Yan*, occasionally pierced by angry shouts that could be ascribed to the immoderate consumption of beer. The mayhem began every morning at six and went on until midnight. It was enough to drive anybody insane—and Ann Randall's sanity hung by such a fine thread she was like one of those cartoon characters holding on to the cliff's edge with a shaky index finger.

Her anxiety steadily mushroomed, until, one night in July, everything collapsed.

Hope was drifting between two phases of sleep when she was awakened by the clink of dishes. Someone was rummaging around in the cupboards. She edged her way to the kitchen, which she found in state of total chaos. Her mother was frantically emptying the fridge.

"What are you doing, Mom?"

Ann Randall turned around with a start, looking like a burglar caught red-handed. She stared at her daughter for a moment and, unable to recognize her, continued to empty the fridge.

"I'm packing."

"To go where?"

"West."

Ann Randall truly believed that she could gain some time by escaping toward the west, perhaps by virtue of the clock's reversal as one travelled westward through the time zones. Even more likely, however, was that her thinking was based on an abstruse biblical interpretation of the cardinal points or on the lyrics of a Led Zeppelin song that she had heard on the radio earlier that night. There was no way of knowing.

Hope acquiesced, getting out of her pyjamas and putting on the first clothes she could find: an old pair of ripped jeans, a T-shirt and a New York Mets baseball cap. She wistfully packed her bag, managing to jam in a half-dozen volumes of her Russian textbooks. She took a last look inside the closet—the small cocoon furnished with her books, her TV, her cushions, her David Suzuki posters. She sighed. Why hadn't she been born into a family obsessed by deer hunting, the Super Bowl or municipal politics?

In the kitchen, her mother had almost finished emptying the fridge. She thrust a bag of provisions into Hope's arms.

"Here, go put this in the car."

Hope reluctantly obeyed. In front of the house their ancient Lada was waiting, all its doors open. It was an ailing, second-hand car purchased the year before with the family's meagre savings. The trunk overflowed with bags, knick-knacks, clothing. Ann Randall had even jettisoned the spare tire to make room for her bible collection. Every seat except the driver's was laden with boxes, and the floor was covered with sacks of flour, boxes of ramen, jars of relish, bottles of vinegar, ketchup and soy sauce, jars of mustard.

Hope looked at the poor Lada with its sunken shock absorbers. Anything over thirty kilometres per hour might be too much to expect of it.

She returned inside, grabbed her bag and hurried to the bathroom. In the medicine cabinet were rows of clozapine, twenty-odd bottles. Suddenly she heard the noise of a car door slamming shut. Ann Randall had just sat down behind the steering wheel. Hope tossed the drugs into her bag, fished out the prescription (folded twelve times) from under the jar of Vaseline and raced back to the car before her mother got a notion to take off on her own.

The Scotiabank clock showed 4 a.m. and 12°C as the two women pulled out of Yarmouth doing 55 kilometres an hour and equipped with a thermos of reddish tea and a road map that was torn along the boundary between Maine and Témiscouata.

Curled up in a corner of the back seat, Hope tried to catch up on her night's sleep. She rested her head against the backpack, with the bottles of clozapine shaking next to her ear like maracas.

When she woke up it was midmorning and they were in the depths of New Brunswick. Her mother had taken the logging road that sliced the province in half—an endless stretch of gravel flanked by thousands of hectares of spruce bearing the Irving dynasty's coat of arms. For two hours they encountered nothing but convoys of logging trucks and dusty 4x4s. They emerged somewhere in the northwest of the province and crossed the border into Témiscouata, where the yellow haze of forest fires hung in the air. Overhead, CL-215s roared back and forth.

Hope spoke not a word, immersed in her Russian studies. She knew that her questions would elicit nothing but vague theological gibberish. In any case, the one question that really mattered was how long would they keep on driving like this? Only the mighty Pacific itself could stop Ann Randall, and even then she was quite capable of plowing headlong into the ocean. Some action would have to be taken, but what could Hope do? She had five thousand kilometres to figure something out.

But then this happened: Comrade Lada's heart abruptly gave out among the peat bogs a few kilometres south of Rivière-du-Loup, struck down (as it were) by fate. A breakdown of this magnitude could not be ascribed to mechanics but only to karma: five valves overheating at once, the carburetor reduced to mush, gears unhinged and countless nuts and bolts gone AWOL.

The repairman who came to their aid chewed his toothpick thoughtfully as he examined the vehicle. Then he passed sentence: Kaput! They were better off selling the carcass by the kilo than wasting another minute on the case.

Ann Randall, who had calmed down somewhat over the twelve-hour drive, took stock of the situation. To go back was out of the question. She asked the mechanic a few questions about Rivière-du-Loup and straightaway deemed it a suitable place to wait for the end of the world.

They rented the former pet shop located near the kitchen vent of the Chinese Garden Restaurant, Serving Chinese and Canadian Food. With a considerable portion of their savings having gone toward the first month's rent, Ann had to take a job at a warehouse in the industrial park, where a battalion of hapless souls stuffed paper into knapsacks made in the People's Republic of China. The work was dreary but adequate. After all, the world would soon witness the total annihilation of all modern civilization, the People's Republic of China included.

Ann Randall teetered on the brink of the precipice, always a hair's breadth away from a relapse that was forestalled only by a minute detail of which she was entirely unaware—each morning Hope dissolved two tablets of clozapine in her mother's tea.

8. EINSTEIN'S TWENTY-FIVE SUITS

On the morning of the first day of school I knocked on the door of the Pet Shop. Hope's mother had just left, and the only sign of her presence was a heap of warm blankets on the sofa bed. Which didn't really bother me, as I was in no particular hurry to make the acquaintance of this psychiatric specimen.

On the way to school, Hope snatched a newspaper peeking out from someone's mailbox. The front page had a picture of Neptune taken by the *Voyager 2* space probe. Hope must have found my enthusiasm wanting, because she proceeded to explain that the probe had been launched in 1977 and the twelve years needed to reach Neptune vividly demonstrated both the vastness of the universe and the extreme smallness of our own planet.

Seen in this light, the new school year appeared pretty insignificant. Score a point for astronomy.

The high school atrium was teeming with people. Classes were about to begin and two thousand students crowded around the stairways. Hope and I huddled in a quiet corner and watched the throng. From time to time

I pointed out a teacher who was either worthy of interest or not to be trusted. Hope asked me if there was anyone I wanted to see.

"No, not really."

Which meant, of course, that for the moment there was no one more important than Hope.

We folded our arms and surveyed the students as they bustled about with their new outfits, elaborate hairstyles and finely tuned slang. I casually noted that Hope had been wearing the same clothes for a week: an old pair of torn jeans, a frayed cap and a grey T-shirt. But were they in fact the same? Maybe she was simply emulating Albert Einstein, who, as legend had it, acquired twenty-five identical suits to spare himself the daily bother of deciding what to put on.

The anecdote made Hope smile. She happened to know a thing or two about the life of the great physicist. For example, Einstein had *indeed* sent President Roosevelt a letter urging him to develop the atom bomb before the Germans did. He *actually* had been a socialist Zionist and turned down an invitation to become president of Israel in 1952. And he *really* had stated: "I don't know which arms will be used in the Third World War, but the fourth will be fought with linoleum cutters bought at the local Home Hardware."

And yet Hope had never heard the story of the twenty-five identical suits.

The fact was, she always wore the same things because they were the only clothes she had managed to grab before leaving Yarmouth. She had been washing her T-shirt and underwear every night in the kitchen sink, but after three weeks of this routine she admitted that she would soon have to find another solution.

Maybe it was time to consider the Albert Einstein Method.

9. THE LAST GREAT MANIA

By the autumn equinox Hope had so completely adapted to her new ecosystem that anyone would have believed she had always lived here. Even her funny accent was somewhat less conspicuous. Still, she continued to sleep in the bathtub, which did nothing to reassure me of the stability of their situation. Whenever I showed up at the Randall Pet Shop, I was afraid of finding it deserted, evacuated due to another flare-up of nocturnal psychosis.

As far as Hope was concerned, there was nothing to worry about. Thanks to the miraculous molecules of clozapine, Mrs. Randall's major phobias had now been reduced to minor and altogether bearable obsessions.

In the meantime the Pet Shop was looking more and more like a den, or a shooting gallery—disposable housing to discard after use. One Saturday morning, while Mrs. Randall was away, Hope and I confronted the mess head-on. While I swept up, Hope piled dishes in the sink filled with soapy water. A few bubbles floated around the Pet Shop, reflecting everything around them—miniature backup copies of our universe.

Hope had strictly forbidden me to touch the kitchen table, which sagged under a thick layer of paperwork: equations, lunar phases, kabbalistic diagrams and Captain Mofuku ramen packages. This jumble represented the last great mania, which the clozapine had not managed to subdue: Mrs. Randall persisted in searching for the date of the end of the world.

In her view, the situation was perfectly clear: if the apocalypse had failed to take place during the summer of 1989 as predicted, then the calendar must be at fault. All her evenings were devoted to solving this problem. She converted the Julian calendar into the Hebrew calendar and vice versa, claimed that here and there a handful of leap years had not been factored in, fumed at Gregory XIII, cursed the incompetent astronomer who in 1847 had misplaced a comma.

No doubt about it, Mrs. Randall was off her rocker. Hope shrugged indulgently.

"It's something you can't understand. A Randall finds comfort in knowing exactly when the world will end. The date is a marker. It gives you the impression you've got everything under control."

This explanation disturbed me. Since Hope had not yet experienced her Spell from Hell, did it mean she was tormented by the idea of not knowing the date of the apocalypse?

She burst out laughing. How could Mary Hope Juliet Randall—that hard-core admirer of David Suzuki, that wizard of algebra and molecular chemistry—how could she possibly subscribe to such medieval notions? Please!

I dropped the subject and resumed sweeping up my pile of crumbs, but for a long while Hope appeared troubled. I had obviously hit a nerve.

10. COLD FUSION

In early October, Hope took it into her head to save some money for her personal use. After badgering the district manager for three weeks, she finally persuaded him to assign her a newspaper delivery route. It was an almost miraculous accomplishment at the time, as such routes were jealously guarded preserves, passed on exclusively from father to son and brother to brother.

As she trekked from bungalow to bungalow every morning with a heavy satchel bouncing on her hip, Hope would read the paper, adroitly unfolded to the international news section. Then, looking like a chimney sweep, she would return to the Pet Shop, shower, eat breakfast, spike her mother's tea and, at 7:30 on the dot, knock on our door.

One day, she showed up thirty minutes earlier than usual, her nose smudged with ink, her backpack hanging over one shoulder and a towel around her neck.

"Did you know that the main ingredient of printing ink is soya oil?"

"Oh?"

"Which is why it's virtually impossible to remove without hot water and soap."

"Oh. I see. Problems with your plumbing?"

"Our shower spits huge clots of rust. Usually I just thump the wall to unblock the artery, but this morning, nothing works. Is it okay if I wash up quickly?"

Of course she could. I showed her to the bathroom in the basement. But was that story about soya oil for real? Hope assured me it was. Soya oil had replaced petroleum oil in the 1970s during the OPEC embargo. I sometimes wondered what Gutenberg might have thought of our civilization.

Hope shut herself in the bathroom while I tried to finish my math homework. The last problem—an especially nasty equation with three unknowns—was giving me a hard time, but there was absolutely no way I could concentrate. My attention was entirely bent toward the hiss of the shower on the other side of the bathroom door. I tried to focus on the page, but it was no use. I started thinking about X-rays. My mind set to work on the wall, piercing the atoms, penetrating the prefab panels, the wood, the steam, and mapping out Hope's slender silhouette lathering under the shower.

I was still struggling with my equation when Hope emerged from the bathroom ten minutes later, barefoot. She wore a pair of jeans and a Goldorak T-shirt that was a little too small for her—this didn't help me at all. (She had recently picked up a bagful of children's clothes at the Saint Vincent de Paul thrift store.)

She walked around the basement while she dried the nape of her neck, paused to glance at the TV, and then stopped to scrutinize the large photo of my aunt Ida posing proudly in front of the family fleet of cement trucks. Hope stooped down to read the little bronze plaque: *Bétons Bauermann Inc.—Fiers Bâtisseurs Depuis 1953.*

Hope stepped toward me with her towel wrapped caliph-style around her head.

"Algebra problems?"

I grunted. She grabbed a pencil and, drying her hair with her other hand, cleaned up my calculations. In a few seconds the unknowns gave way to an elegant solution. Then she gestured with her chin at the picture of my aunt Ida.

"Your family is in concrete?"

I smiled. My family was indeed in concrete. Just as Hope was pressing me for more information, my mother arrived at the top of the stairs to ask if we felt like waffles. An altogether rhetorical question. I promised Hope to disclose all the facts on the Bauermann tribe, but some other day. We went upstairs.

The kitchen was filled with a sugary aroma. Laid out on the table were a basket of freshly microwaved waffles, some oranges and a pitcher of corn syrup. My father was reading the business section of the paper, while my mother perused the obituaries. The coffee maker was hard at work and the muted radio provided some ambient noise.

My father, obviously in a good mood, addressed Hope in a booming voice.

"Well, what's new, Miss Randall?"

Hope beamed a huge smile in his direction and speared three waffles.

"The usual. Major riots in Leipzig in protest against the Communist regime. Oh, and cold fusion has apparently turned out to be a load of bull."

I studied my parents' faces while she spread a kilo of Nutella on her waffles. Father: amused. Mother: bewildered. My mother folded the newspaper and swept away a few crumbs with the back of her hand.

"And how is your mother?"

"Okay, I guess. She works a lot. Doesn't eat well. But if you *really* want my opinion, none of that's as interesting as cold fusion."

11. PERFECTLY LIVABLE FOR EXTENDED PERIODS

Hope was spending more and more time in our basement. Given the rather peculiar atmosphere at the Randall Pet Shop, I couldn't blame her. She needed a change of scenery, so her Russian textbooks gathered dust while we spent all of our evenings ensconced in the huge, squashy sofa, watching TV with a bowl of pretzels close by.

The Nature of Things having just ended, we slipped into a slight trough, as we always did on Friday nights. For Hope, no act was worthy of following *sensei* Suzuki.

Flipping through the channels, I found a BBC report on the archaeological dig at Pompeii. Hope pretended to pay attention only when the commercials were on— probably just to infuriate me. At every commercial break she would go into raptures, act as if she were in a trance or search for coded messages in the tampon ads (maximum freedom, supreme comfort).

Why is archaeology so underrated?

In Pompeii, the sun was beating down on a group of poorly paid trainees who scraped the ground with trowels and brushes. An Italian archaeologist pointed out one of the site's particularities: The excavation occasionally uncovered hollows left by the victims' bodies. By simply pouring plaster into one of these cavities and later prying the cast free with a chisel, they could obtain a 3-D Polaroid of a Pompeii inhabitant at the exact moment of death. (This detail briefly snagged Hope's attention.)

The camera ranged over a warehouse filled with dozens of such castings. Shelves upon shelves of asphyxiated Roman citizens—recumbent, curled up, snuggling against each other—an entire population turned into concrete.

I wondered if the eruption of Vesuvius had surprised some Pompeians in a final act of copulation and, if so, whether the archaeologists had managed to make convincing casts of these events.

Hope yawned and scratched her navel. She stretched out her arm only to find a few grains of coarse salt at the bottom of the bowl.

"Any pretzels left?"

I handed her the bag. The TV showed walls covered with ancient graffiti. The Romans hadn't waited for the invention of spray paint to vandalize public spaces. Hope got up and started wandering around the basement while she rummaged in the bag of pretzels. She paused to look at the picture of my aunt Ida and the cement trucks, and then planted herself in front of my sci-fi novels.

"Have you read all of them?"

I nodded. She wiped her hands on her jeans, pulled out an Isaac Asimov title and leafed through it.

"Where do you buy them?"

"At Youri's. It's a bookstore on Lafontaine Street."

She examined the bookshelves from top to bottom until she was kneeling in front of the archaeology section at floor level. Predictably, the contrast made her smile. For Hope, as for most of my peers, it was difficult to recognize the natural connection between science fiction and archaeology.

The report on Pompeii was finishing and Hope immediately insisted on watching the news. I switched channels just in time to catch veteran anchorman Bernard Derome announcing the top stories. Keywords: devastating, typhoon, Thailand.

Gay was the most powerful typhoon to hit the Malaysian peninsula in decades. There were winds approaching 200 kilometres an hour, and we watched a little house get blown out to sea like a cardboard box. It was enough to send shivers up your spine. Would our bungalow have fared any better?

"Interesting question," Hope murmured.

She looked around the basement and stated that, when you thought about it, the North American bungalow shared certain characteristics with a bunker. It was one of the only modern dwellings where fifty per cent of the living space was located *below* ground level.

"Previously, houses had cellars, crypts, underground rooms, crawl spaces or secret vaults for storing Kalashnikovs. But the basement of a North American bungalow is different. It's insulated, heated, furnished, equipped with beds, freezers, cold-storage rooms, a television, a telephone and board games."

"Not to mention the angora rug!"

"Not to mention the angora rug . . . In other words, it's perfectly livable for extended periods."

As she spoke, Hope fished out a stray pretzel from between two sofa cushions.

"The modern basement appeared during the Cold War. It's the product of a civilization obsessed with its future. But when you think about it, you have to go back to the Stone Age to find so many *Homo sapiens* living underground."

She tossed the pretzel into the air. It described a perfect parabola before landing between her teeth. Crunch.

"In conclusion, modernity is a fairly relative concept."

Hope—wow.

She fell asleep during the weather report, head thrown back, muttering incomprehensibly. I turned down the TV, spread a blanket over her legs and watched her sleep for a moment.

The human brain is said to consume one-fifth of the energy produced by the body, but Hope's brain clearly burned up much more. She was breathing quietly. I shut my eyes and imagined her cortex silently splitting pellets of uranium-235.

12. TERMITES

We caught the last rays of the autumn sun as we sat shivering in the bleachers of the municipal stadium. We were already wearing tuques and coats as protection against the icy wind rising from the river. With such cold weather in early November, the threat of a new ice age could not be shrugged off. I had rifled through my brother's dresser and dug up an old down parka that was just slightly too big. Bundled up in the bulky red jacket, Hope looked like a little girl, but she didn't seem to mind.

For weeks she had been demanding a General History of the Bauermann Family—including both fact and lore—so with chattering teeth I was now about to indulge her curiosity.

My forebears left the Netherlands in the middle of the nineteenth century and settled in New Jersey, where they worked as masons, becoming gradually more specialized in cement and concrete. Their success was such that on the eve of the Second World War they ran one of the region's largest cement companies: the Bauermann Portland Cement Works.

The plant was located beside the Fresh Kills River, a stone's throw from what would one day become the world's biggest garbage dump. The biggest factories, the largest dumps—America, the promised land.

The Bauermanns' golden age came to an end in the early years of the Cold War, when the family was pushed out of the local market by the Mafia. Of course, they tried to stand their ground, but after dozens of battles on the construction sites, death threats, sudden boycotts and a considerable number of truck windshields shattered by baseball bats, my venerable grandfather, Wilhelm Bauermann, decided to leave to other visionaries the task of building New York.

The exodus of the Bauermanns took place on a December morning in 1953. The family convoy stretched over several kilometres of Interstate 87: cement trucks, crushers, washers and, above all, a monumental kiln resting on two drays.

"A *what*?"

"A kiln. It's a rotating oven. It looks like a large, sloping pipe. Raw material goes in one end, clinker comes out at the other, and the oven can operate day and night, non-stop."

"Fascinating."

"May I continue?"

"Please do."

So, the Bauermanns travelled up into New England, crossed into Canada and stopped at Rivière-du-Loup in an embryonic industrial park a few kilometres from the soon-to-be-built Autoroute 20. Lots of overpasses on the horizon.

Canadian garbage dumps were not as extensive as the American ones, and the factories were smaller. So the Bauermann family scaled down its ambitions. My uncle Kurt would sometimes reminisce about growing up in New Jersey, the giant plant that never slept, the constant traffic of cement trucks, the groan of the kilns and especially the mountains of coal, which, from the top, offered a view of the Manhattan skyline veiled in mist like the Baghdad of *A Thousand and One Nights*.

Our family kept on grinding out cement. The Bauermanns' destiny was traced out as clearly as the path of a termite colony: my father ran the cement plant, my uncle Kurt managed the concrete plant and my legendary aunt Ida commanded the fleet of cement trucks. She's the one posing in that famous picture in our basement: arms folded, standing like a rock in front of a half-circle of enormous chrome-plated Mack trucks. Whenever I want to conjure up the image of the conquistador Hernán Cortés,

I think of that pose of Aunt Ida's. Watch out, New World.

Hope laughed. Wasn't I overstating the case just a little? No, I was not. For the Bauermanns, concrete wasn't just a business; it was a matter of civilization, a mission to be passed on from father to son. We were builders of worlds.

"So you plan to take over the factory?"

She'd hit on a sensitive subject—the Bauermanns' calling was in jeopardy. Neither Kurt nor Ida had produced offspring, and my brother had just committed treason by going off to study psychology—my father was still reeling from that blow. As the youngest, the onus of delivering the coup de grâce would fall to me, and I dreaded the day when I would have to announce my intention of studying comparative literature rather than strapping on the harness.

The expression on Hope's face changed abruptly. She turned toward the bungalows and looked worried, or cross. Just as I was about to ask her what the matter was, hailstones began to pop all around us. Within seconds the storm came crashing down on our heads.

We ran down to the dugout for shelter.

The squall was violent and abrupt. It was impossible to make our voices heard above the din of hail striking the roof of the dugout. The pits in the baseball field soon overflowed with millions of hailstones as immaculate as Styrofoam beads.

Hope looked on, lost in thought. The latter part of my story had evidently annoyed her, and it was not hard to figure out where I had blundered. I had complained about a situation that Hope envied: my father cared about me, had expectations, was interested in my future, even though that future—unfortunately for me—came in the shape of an obsolete cement plant in a remote corner of the country.

As for Mrs. Randall, she nurtured no dreams for her daughter. Hope could become a stripper, a Pentecostal preacher or a cashier at a McDonald's—it didn't make the slightest difference.

13. PLEASE AVOID THE VERBS *TO BE* AND *TO HAVE*

A Friday like so many others, after school.

The moment I arrived at the Bunker—the nickname that Hope had affectionately given our basement—I switched on the mighty Mac SE and flung my bag down on the floor. It popped open wide enough for a few sheets of paper to spill out, including the instructions for our composition assignment. The topic was rather all-encompassing: "What will the world of tomorrow look like?" Suggested length: 250 words. Please avoid the verbs *to be* and *to have*.

I thought about Mrs. Michaud's enthusiasm as she

announced the guidelines, her face beaming with the certainty that this was a harmless creative exercise. She clearly expected the usual clichés: space tourism, household robots, anti-cancer pills.

I stared at the monitor for a minute, sighed, and retreated to the couch, where a comic book lay in tatters: *Godzilla King of the Monsters Meets Captain America*. I flipped it open randomly to an ad for Amazing X-Ray Vision Glasses, capable of penetrating solid matter (including women's clothes) and available at the ridiculous price of $2 USD. Send money order and coupon to Post Box 245, Navajo Creek, Nevada.

The biggest joke since perpetual motion.

A draft swept through the room. Hope was entering the Bunker by the back door (she had given up knocking). No doubt coming over to write her composition on the computer. And—surprise—she was carrying an old red sleeping bag under her arm, obviously intending to spend the night. I immediately presumed the worst. She chucked her things in a corner.

"Have you been following the news?"

I shook my head—I knew nothing of the latest tremors affecting Nicaraguan domestic politics, the Bank of Tokyo or Lebanon's groundwater supply. Unimpressed by my attempt at humour, she switched on the television and plunked down beside me. On the screen, an unbelievable event was unfolding: hundreds of people dancing and hugging on top of what looked to me like an old concrete warehouse.

Hope turned toward me. Her eyes sparkled electric blue.

"The Berlin Wall has just come down!"

14. *GRENZMAUER*

In the wake of an amusing slip committed by a high-ranking leader, the GDR had just allowed its citizens to circulate between the East and the West at certain crossings, and was preparing to open the wall at a dozen more locations. We were witnessing a live broadcast of a historic point of no return. Berliners in droves revelled, crossed checkpoints and attacked the wall with whatever tools they had: hammers, sledgehammers and all manner of battering rams. A surge of optimism to warm the heart.

In front of the Brandenburg Gate, a backhoe sent a section of wall crashing down onto the pavement. The Wall wasn't falling; it was toppling over, and with mind-boggling ease. So a nudge from a bulldozer was all it took to dispose of this shameful structure? I watched with growing fascination as the Wall collapsed again and again.

The Iron Curtain had been slapped together with Gyproc. According to Hope, the truth was actually a lot simpler. It was a wall made of Lego blocks.

"Lego blocks?"

"Reinforced concrete Lego blocks, a metre wide and four metres tall, with a T-shaped base. This wall is the fourth generation—the *Grenzmauer 75* model. Architecture that's modular, grey and efficient."

The daily dose of useless information.

On the TV screen, sections of wall were tumbling at a brisk pace, and I wondered what the Germans planned to do with all those Lego blocks cluttering up Berlin. Hope predicted that the value of a Genuine Fragment of Wall would rise briefly on the local market before plummeting throughout the free world.

"They'll of course try to sell entire sections as trophies in the U.S."

She was even willing to bet five dollars on the following scenario: A wealthy businessman would quickly step in and buy the whole wall in order to secure a monopoly (the current regime would be happy to turn a profit from what otherwise was shaping up to be a costly historical episode). Said businessman would then hire a container ship and move the wall, piece by duly numbered piece, to the suburbs of Orlando, where he would wage a terrific competitive war with Walt Disney World.

I tried to picture what such a *Mauerland* might look like. Dismal.

The same backhoe continued to topple the same section of wall in front of the Brandenburg Gate. As recent as it was, history was already running in a loop. Hope seemed to be assessing the weight of a piece of the *Grenzmauer* and the cost of shipping it via marine cargo. Then she spotted the comic book on the coffee table opened at the ad for the Amazing X-Ray Vision Glasses. She scanned the advertisement, raising an eyebrow. I anticipated her sarcasm.

"I know. You're going to say that it violates every law of modern physics . . ."

"Actually, I was wondering why guys don't try to simply persuade girls to undress instead of ordering these stupid gadgets. Though I admit that for two dollars I wouldn't take off very much."

She wriggled her toes inside her woollen socks as though estimating the market value of her feet.

The TV reporter was remembering the Wall's 140 victims over the years when my mother appeared with a basketful of dirty laundry. As she greeted Hope, the red sleeping bag instantly flashed on her radar screen. Red alert.

She positioned herself behind us with the laundry basket perched on her hip and pretended to take an interest in what was happening on the screen, where the section of wall kept tipping over. Finally, she coughed a little to draw our attention.

"Hope, am I to understand that you're going to spend the night here?"

"If it's no bother."

"I would be more concerned about it bothering your mother, don't you think?"

Hope's almost playful response was that there was really nothing to worry about. My mother was not reassured. Out of the corner of my eye I saw her lift the receiver and dial the Pet Shop's newly acquired phone number.

Through an extraordinary twist of fate, Mrs. Randall happened to be at home.

Following the conventional courtesies, my mother explained the reason for her call. She had not uttered more than a few syllables when Mrs. Randall took control of the conversation, with my mother barely managing to stammer "yes, yes" or "no, no."

I watched her expression shift from politeness through the whole spectrum of disbelief, to incomprehension and finally to total stupefaction. She hung up and, without saying another word, vanished with her laundry basket. But at suppertime she brought us Chinese food and a family-size bottle of Star Cola, and we ate as we continued to watch Berlin rejoice.

I had no idea what Mrs. Randall had said to my mother, but she never again raised any objections when Hope showed up at the Bunker at all hours of the day or night to eat, sleep, work, read, shower or hang out. My favourite refugee had just been granted permanent residency status.

15. KABOOM!

We spent the evening listening to the news reports while taking turns typing our essays during the commercial breaks. I felt uninspired and fell back on a familiar subject: concrete. I predicted the advent of a revolutionary architecture based on completely new varieties of additives. (In the vocabulary of science fiction, I felt that the word *additive* had a persuasive ring to it.)

Hope, meanwhile—always in sync with current events—foresaw the fall of the Soviet regime and the end of the Cold War within two years. In addition, she wrote, instead of the atomic bomb we would soon start living in fear of the industrial obsolescence of the USSR, as illustrated by the Chernobyl disaster. This new peril would be far greater than the H-bomb; it would be a self-destructive device beyond anyone's control, a time bomb plugged into the very heart of *Imperium Sovieticum*.

Her miniature essay (250 words exactly) was succinctly entitled "Kaboom!"

As the StyleWriter spat out our papers, Hope asked me for an unbiased opinion. I mechanically corrected a few spelling mistakes and said that it was a very good paper that would most likely earn her a very poor mark. The mere idea of Mrs. Michaud's horrified expression made me laugh.

We watched the last news broadcast, and then the stations signed off one by one. Toward midnight, the choice came down to David Letterman's *Late Night*, *L'Île des passions* and the eight-hundredth rerun of *Planet of the Apes*.

Naturally, we opted for *Planet of the Apes*.

16. THE DAWN OF A NEW ERA

The atrium was teeming with the usual Monday-morning commotion. There was no sign whatsoever that the Berlin Wall had come down just a few days before. The high school was history-proof.

Going up the stairs, we bumped into Mr. Chénard, who was toting a paper bag full of lemons.

Chénard had been teaching chemistry for decades. He was born during the Great Depression—i.e., prehistoric times—making him the oldest teacher in the school, an inexhaustible fount of anecdotes and the butt of many a cheap joke.

Hope liked him in the way one is fond of a grandfather who survived World War Two. She often hung out in his office during lunch hour. As Chénard filled his pipe with two or three pinches of cheap tobacco, she would rest her feet on the edge of his desk, and they would discuss Darwinism, geology and quantum physics. On a shelf, a shortwave radio played quietly. This was no mere appliance, but its owner's alter ego, a venerable tube radio that in days gone by had tuned in to Eisenhower and Orson Welles. Now, all it could pull in was the local AM station.

So Chénard was coming down the stairs on the wrong side, the bag full of lemons clutched against his stained lab coat, pipe wedged behind his ear. He said hello and exchanged a few words with Hope on the subject of Berlin.

"How old were you in 1945, Mr. Chénard?" she asked abruptly.

Caught off guard, he raised his eyebrows.

"About fourteen."

"So do you remember Hiroshima?"

"The bomb? Yes, I remember it."

He seemed pensive as he settled the bag of lemons on his hip.

"Yes, I remember the bomb," he repeated.

A wave of students rolled by on the port and starboard

sides of us, grumbling at the obstacle that we were creating, and our old chemistry teacher suddenly resembled one of those figures in a movie standing still in a public place while hundreds of extras rush past in accelerated motion. But Chénard was only outwardly immobile—under the surface, his mind was racing back through time at the speed of light.

"What I remember most are the newspapers. The tone was . . . triumphant."

"*Triumphant?*" I exclaimed.

"Indeed. Canada had taken part in the Manhattan Project. They were proclaiming the dawn of a new era. Houses heated with atomic energy. Plutonium-fuelled cars. An unlimited source of power. It made me want to study science."

He absently watched the students streaming past on either side, as though suddenly waking in the middle of a flood. He blinked his eyes, as if searching for an explanation.

"You know, a lot of scientists found their calling with Hiroshima."

The first-period bell rang. As if waiting for a signal, the paper bag on Mr. Chénard's hip split open. Dozens of lemons tumbled down the stairs, bouncing around the students' ankles.

We hurried off to class, leaving him to deal with his citruses. But Hope was intrigued.

"What do you think he's going to do with those lemons?"

17. MEGALEMONS

As a worthy bearer of the Randall name, Hope never let go of an obsession. She twisted and turned it in every direction like a Rubik's cube and could keep this up in the background for hours, sometimes days. I watched her spend the day sketching the outlines of variously sized lemons on her desk, in the margins of her English notebook, on the palm of her hand.

The mystery was cleared up in the late afternoon in the chemistry lab. Mr. Chénard was going to teach us how to use lemons to put together an electric battery.

The experiment seemed perfectly straightforward. All it required was to stick two electrodes into the unfortunate fruit and, with the aid of a voltmeter, note the very faint electrical current generated by the potential difference. The current was just barely perceptible—around 1.5 volts—so several hundred lemons would have to be hooked up in series for a 40-watt bulb to light up. Of course, the main point of the experiment was not to produce electricity but to explain the role that citric acid, zinc and aluminum played in this curious phenomenon.

Hope and I made a formidable team—admittedly, thanks mostly to Hope—and we completed the experiment in no time. I was already proofreading our report while our closest neighbours were still struggling with their prescribed fruit, trying in vain to lance the peel with the copper wire.

Armed with a scalpel, Hope proceeded to dissect our lemon.

"Do you know the origin of the word 'electricity'?"

"No idea."

"The Greeks discovered static electricity by rubbing a piece of amber against some fur. In Greek, 'electron' means amber."

Hope's face puckered as she bit into a lemon wedge.

"Can you imagine what would have happened if they'd been fiddling around with citrus fruits? Everything would have another name. We would be taking courses in citricity, and the lemon would be an official unit of electric measurement!"

"That's pretty absurd."

"Yeah, but *all* units of measurement are absurd. It doesn't matter if you measure time with drops of water or the rotations of a cesium atom—both are merely absurdities with different degrees of accuracy. Everything else is cultural."

Right then I observed a sparkle of excitement in her eyes. She opened her chemistry textbook to the conversion tables and began jotting down notes in the margins of the book and punching numbers into her calculator.

"What are you doing?"

"I'm converting the Hiroshima atomic bomb into lemons."

Of course. What could be more obvious?

Hope explained that all you needed was a little logic and a smattering of data to obtain a significant, if not altogether exact, answer. In other words, the renowned Fermi method.

In this particular case, you could start with the fact that a lemon contains 15 to 20 calories, that is (she tapped away on her calculator) an average value of 73.2 kilojoules (x). The Hiroshima bomb, on the other hand, released an estimated 15 kilotons of energy, amounting to approximately 6.3×10^{13} kilojoules (y).

To convert the bomb's energy, you had only to divide y by x, which resulted in a total of 8.6×10^{11} lemons or, more plainly, 860,655 megalemons, the equivalent of Florida's agricultural output over a period of six thousand years.

Hope went back to work, calculator in hand, and was now computing the volume 860 billion lemons would take up.

Around us, the other students were busy with their coils of copper wire, their sticky fruits and their stacks of loose-leaf filled with scribbled notes. As for me, I pondered the heresy of converting the deadliest explosion in the history of humankind into lemons.

Yet it was inevitable that it should come to this sooner or later.

For the average citizen in 1945, the atomic bomb came from the future, just like the extraterrestrials in *The War of the Worlds*. While physicists were piercing the core of the atom, people in the countryside were still using oil lamps to light their houses.

My grandfather, Wilhelm Bauermann—who had grown up with the steam engine, mustard gas and the Model T Ford—was unable to grasp that the atomic bomb was fundamentally different from dynamite. When he talked about Hiroshima, he imagined a mountain of those cardboard sticks they used in the gypsum quarries.

The children of the postwar years had witnessed the advent of the Boeing 747, LSD and the H-bomb, and by the time my generation arrived on the scene, 100-kiloton intercontinental missiles already belonged to ancient history. They were like the microwave oven, Captain Mofuku chicken-flavoured ramen or satellite TV—an ordinary component of everyday reality.

No, Grandpa Wilhelm could never have understood how the Hiroshima bomb differed from good old dynamite, and even less how it could be compared to lemons.

19. EINSTEIN WAS WRONG

My parents had gone down to Montreal until Wednesday to take part in the annual convention of North-Eastern Cement Producers—forty-eight hours of scintillating discussions on all the latest additives, the whole event awash in weak coffee and lukewarm beer.

Lounging on the couch with our feet up on the coffee table, Hope and I were doing our best to diminish the reserves of frozen mini-pizzas. While I flipped through the *TV Guide*, Hope kept half an eye on a news report about Berlin. Nothing new under the sun.

I asked about Mrs. Randall: Was she making any headway with the date of the end of the world? Hope sighed. No, her mother was getting nowhere. As a matter of fact, she was showing dangerous signs of restlessness. Hope wondered how much longer the clozapine would continue to keep her condition stable. Fundamentally, the issue was not pharmaceutical. All she needed was to find that date and her mental health would immediately improve.

Hope threw her head back and stared at the ceiling for a long time.

"The problem is in her method. She mixes everything up. Mysticism, bogus mathematics, the Kabala, astrology . . . It lacks elegance."

"Elegance?"

"An old mathematical concept. The more an idea is unnecessarily complicated, the less elegant it is."

"I see. So absolute elegance would look something like $E=mc^2$?"

Hope blinked and sat up with a start.

"Do you have dice?"

Of course I had dice. Every North American home worthy of the name had an old Monopoly game stored away in a closet. It took me two minutes to find ours. Hidden under the bundles of banknotes, property titles and miniature bungalows was a pair of dice. But, as hard as I tried, I could not see the connection with the theory of relativity.

"There's no connection. Except that it reminded me of Einstein's famous statement: 'God does not play with dice.' "

She gave me a lopsided smile.

"But Einstein was wrong. God does play with dice!"

Assembling pen and paper, she drew a grid and wrote down a series of numbers. I tried to follow but lacked some basic data.

"It's simple. I'm going to find the date of the end of the world by chance."

"By chance?"

"Can you think of anything more elegant?"

No, I couldn't. Hope would throw the dice. Even numbers would mean "yes" and odd numbers would mean "no." This simplest of conventions would allow her to determine the date through a process of elimination.

The dice clattered across the coffee table. I loved that sound. It took me back to my childhood when my family would spend entire evenings around the Monopoly board. It had been years since we last played, and it felt rather bizarre, in hindsight, to picture my family gathered around a small-scale model of the world, taking part in simulated financial wars.

While I daydreamed, Hope tossed the dice. Between throws, she wrote certain numbers down and crossed out others. This method was not only elegant but quick, and two minutes were enough for her to determine that the apocalypse would happen on July 17, 2001.

Well, at least that was one thing out of the way!

Now we could look forward to spending a quiet evening.

Hope said nothing. She was testing the date in her head, running her mind over it as if it were the sharp edge of a knife.

"Not a very credible date, is it?"

I shrugged my shoulders, preferring to let the Randalls form an opinion on the matter. Hope looked at the dice resting innocently in the palm of her hand. There was no question of a computational error; that was the whole advantage—and absurdity—of chance.

"And why exactly do you find that July 17, 2001, lacks credibility?"

"*July!* Can you really imagine the apocalypse happening during the construction holiday?"

To tell the truth, yes, I had no trouble conjuring up this image—but maybe I'd just read too much science fiction.

"Okay, fine. July's no good. So which month *would* you see it occurring?"

She mulled over the question. Clearly, April, May and June were out. A springtime doomsday could simply not be taken seriously. August and September were lame choices—the end of the world would look like an ad campaign. "Super-Powerful Armageddon, 20% more Ammonia!" Ridiculous. October, in a pinch, could qualify. In November, on the other hand, the end of days would seem redundant. Any time during the winter could fit the bill, so long as it didn't fall during the holidays.

Sitting with her arms folded, Hope cast a disgruntled look at the dice. What good was it resorting to chance if you couldn't manage to trust it?

I watched her grapple with her internal contradictions. This chink in her self-assurance brought to light a more human, more feminine Hope. Who would have thought that doubt could be so sexy?

20. *TORA! TORA! TORA!*

Surfing the channels, we came across the second half of a film about Pearl Harbor. Instant consensus. Tucked under three old sleeping bags—relics of those sunny days when my family partook of the joys of camping—we watched the screaming Zeroes swoop down on the Pacific Fleet. On the deck of the warship, a brass band hastily finished playing "The Star-Spangled Banner." It was the sort of ludicrous scene that we relished.

Just as the USS *California* was being blown up, Hope cried out, "What about December?"

"What?"

While the debris was raining down on the harbour, the

Zeroes launched another volley of torpedoes. We could actually smell the stench of diesel.

"In December. The end of the world. Just like the attack on Pearl Harbor. Not bad, eh?"

My response has been lost to history.

The news came on immediately after the film. The Lebanese president René Moawad had been killed in a bomb attack and we were seeing the first pictures to arrive from Beirut. In the bright sunshine, a mushroom of black smoke rose high into the sky. Hope frowned. On second thought, the summertime could prove as likely a moment as any for the world to end.

We pulled the plug on the television around midnight and bedded down where we lay, wrapped in the sleeping bags that reeked of mothballs, using cushions for pillows.

It took me a long time to drift off, due to the disturbing effect of Hope lying so close, with her back to me and her body pressing into mine. I finally managed to fall asleep, only to wake up in the middle of the night. The VCR clock showed 2:37 a.m., and I realized that Hope was no longer beside me. She was sitting on the couch, gnawing at her fingernails.

"Can't sleep?"

She shook her head.

"What do you think of February?"

I was speechless for a moment as my neurons revved up one by one.

"No better or worse than any other month."

She sighed.

"No. That's not it. It feels too contrived. So . . . are you hungry?"

By way of response, my stomach rumbled loudly.

We went on a supply raid in the kitchen, where I knew the location of the reserves of chicken-flavoured Captain Mofuku ramen. Genuine bunker food—non-perishable and mould proof. The package design, on the other hand, was a hazard for the eyes: a pink and yellow astronaut with a cretinous smile behind his visor, orbiting a planet made of noodles. True, this was bunker food, but anyone stuck forty metres below ground surrounded by shelves stacked full of these obnoxious astronauts was in danger of losing his mind before succumbing to malnutrition.

We opened the ramen packages and put the kettle on to boil. Hope fidgeted with the empty wrapper while she continued to ruminate.

"What about March?"

I hesitated. It wouldn't work. March was the Ayers Rock of the calendar—an enormous red, smooth month stranded in the middle of nowhere. Hope nodded.

"You're right."

"Listen . . . why not simply trust the dice?"

Hope didn't answer. Absently, she toyed with her ramen package, folding it over and over with her thumbs. From a distance, she might have been taken for someone playing with a Chinese abacus. Suddenly, she stopped. She smoothed out the wrapper with the edge of her hand and thrust it under my nose, her index finger pointing to where it said, Meilleur Avant—Best Before 2001 17 JUL.

I smiled. An amusing coincidence—that's all. Hope spread her arms out excitedly.

"An amusing coincidence?! Do you have any idea what the odds are for such an *amusing coincidence*?!"

No, I did not have any idea. Nor did Hope, for that matter, but she swore she would calculate it when she had a couple of minutes.

She grabbed the kettle, splashed some boiling water in her bowl, and watched the mushroom cloud of steam rise toward the ceiling. She said no more on the subject of the apocalypse, but folded the wrapper four times and carefully slipped it under her belt.

The weeks passed; winter was fast approaching. In Berlin, sections of the *Grenzmauer* disappeared one after the other and gave way to a long series of vacant lots, promising a spike in real estate speculation. On the Potsdamer Platz, construction cranes were concentrated in numbers unequalled anywhere else in this part of the galaxy. Nothing looked more like the end of a world than the beginning of another.

Meanwhile, Hope was radiant. Her slightest gesture was charged with youthful electricity, as if the little girl that she had never allowed to come out was emerging after a long hibernation. She smiled from morning to night, whistled softly, lobbed snowballs at me—and the girl was a good shot, too.

The December sleet pelted down, and Hope blossomed amid the frost for the pleasure of my eyes alone, since none of my classmates seemed to notice the spectacular transformation. Were they so severely nearsighted that they failed to see how dazzling Hope was? Oh well, their loss was my gain.

Of course, as with all good things, there were some minor annoyances. Hope had taped the treasured Captain Mofuku ramen wrapper inside her locker (beside the picture of David Suzuki) and scribbled the numbers 17 07 2001 everywhere: in the blank spaces of her notebooks, in her books, on her arms, her desk, her jeans, and even in the cafeteria's infamous ravioli sauce.

It was as if the numbers 17 07 2001 no longer represented the date of the apocalypse, and even less the expiry date of a package of ramen, but something like one of those little prayers that Buddhists would copy onto scraps of paper, which they then sent drifting on the four winds.

In the end, though, it was a small price to pay to see Hope so radiant.

Unfortunately, the same could not be said of Mrs. Randall, whose attempts to find fault with the Gregorian calendar had resulted in a long string of failures. The facts had to be faced: the date showing on the calendar was neither May 1988 nor February 1987, but undeniably December 1989.

As a result, she had abruptly lost interest in her calendars and almanacs. But in spite of this, certain clues suggested that she was still not rid of her obsession. Once a Randall, always a Randall. One night, Hope came into the Bunker and handed me a newspaper folded four times.

"I found this under our couch when I was sweeping up."

It was a copy of the *Saint-Laurent*, the local weekly, opened to the classified ads. In the "Cars for Sale" section, a frenzied hand had circled all the clunkers going for under $400.

I didn't know what to make of it, so Hope helped me out: Her mother's obsession had just entered an insidious phase. She would soon start packing provisions and collecting road maps of Western Canada.

"You think she's going to pull up stakes again?"

"I wouldn't be surprised."

"Haven't you been giving her the clozapine every morning?"

"The dosage may not be effective any more. It's happened before."

Hope was at a loss. There was no chance of persuading her mother to consult a specialist, still less of forcing her to do so, and no doctor would sign a prescription without seeing the patient. Hope clearly would have liked for me to come up with a bright idea, but nothing came to mind and she seemed frustrated by my silence. She frowned and stuffed the newspaper into her backpack. She would have to manage on her own—again.

My mother came downstairs holding a basket of dirty laundry against her hip. "For tomorrow's lunch, I put the leftover shepherd's pie in some Tupperware," she announced on her way to the laundry room.

Hope gave me a strange look.

"Your mother makes your lunch?"

"Uh . . . Sometimes. Yeah."

She made a show of disbelief and looked away. On the

television, a preacher was praising the mercy of God Almighty. *Do not suffer alone in your little corner. Come and meet Him. Open your heart, open your eyes. Every answer can be found in the Bible.*

22. *THE ILLUSTRATED ENCYCLOPEDIA OF PSYCHIATRY*

The winter's first snowfall came on a Saturday morning. Objective for the day: produce a diagnosis of Mrs. Randall's mental condition.

As she stepped into the municipal library, Hope cast a sceptical glance at the loans counter, where two aging librarians were filing catalogue cards. In her view, a civilization overly preoccupied with archives was surely a civilization on the decline.

She stationed herself in front of the catalogue and went through the cards in the "Neurology and Psychiatry" section. She jotted down a few interesting call numbers and then, after looking left and right, grabbed a bundle of cards, opened another drawer and planted them haphazardly, like the bulbs of some rare and dangerous plant—the seeds of a new virgin forest.

Her spirits lifted by this small act of terrorism, she scurried away to the stacks.

After leafing through a few works by amateurs, Hope went on to more serious stuff: *The Illustrated Encyclopedia of Psychiatry*, a tome weighing some eight kilos and claiming to cover all the psychological disorders that have afflicted the human race from the Sumerian religious wars to Ronald Reagan's first term in office.

Sitting cross-legged on a chair, Hope spent the whole afternoon combing through the encyclopedia with the aim of identifying the subcategory of fruitcake that her mother belonged to. I had taken refuge in an old *Yoko Tsuno* comic book, but from time to time I would unobtrusively peek over her arm, and what I glimpsed was far from reassuring: an assortment of syndromes, episodes, relapses, phases, differential diagnoses, tricyclic antidepressants, neuroleptics, paranoias, hallucinations and hereditary factors, illustrated here and there with cross-sections of cortex, nebulous graphs and bipolar mice.

For three hours straight, Hope scrutinized this selection from every possible angle, from the Ahenobarbus complex ("variety of pyromania aggravated by an unwholesome attraction to stringed instruments") through to Romero-Ruuk syndrome ("dementia characterized by general muscular rigidity and sudden cannibalistic urges"). She lingered for a while over the highly exotic Type III Jerusalem syndrome ("nervous breakdown experienced by some tourists on their first visit to Jerusalem; those affected believe they are the Messiah, announce the End of Days and are subject to a compulsive need to cut their fingernails"), but finally came to the conclusion that the encyclopedia was outrageously incomplete since there was not a single reference to the malady that dozens of Randalls had endured for seven generations.

By way of revenge, she shelved the encyclopedia over in the children's books section between *Puss in Boots* and *Alice in Wonderland*, raising the prospect of a whole new generation of psychoses.

23. A FAIRLY OPTIMISTIC VIEW OF THE UNIVERSE

Every ten days, religious studies class fell right after phys. ed. The odour of incense and running shoes permeated the hushed classroom where Mr. Bérubé tried (in vain) to inculcate us with a few notions of religious culture. There was something profoundly incompatible between endorphins and theology.

Mr. Bérubé was a young teacher brimming with goodwill. He had taught algebra the year before and would be assigned to home economics the next year. That year, though, he struggled with the recurring peregrinations of a chosen people who, after surviving various enslavements, wandered in the desert and then found itself a disputed messiah, all in thirty-thousand-odd verses. Please follow the official course plan.

Standing in front of a map of Palestine, he announced that the whole class would be devoted to the book of Revelation, also known as the Apocalypse of John, which, as everyone knew, "was a book in the New Testament before becoming a source of inspiration for Iron Maiden!" The joke fell flat.

Mr. Bérubé plunged bravely into his subject. He told us about the Four Horsemen, the Number of the Beast and the Roman occupation in Palestine. Around the classroom, heads were tilted at various angles of repose. I spotted one or two yawns.

Hope, meanwhile, floated light years away from the foul-smelling classroom. She blackened the margins of her notebook with concentric circles and spirals, scribbled time and again the numbers 17 07 2001, like a ray of light glowing out of our dark era.

Mr. Bérubé eagerly shared with us a little-known fact: the Apocalypse was not merely a book in the New Testament but first and foremost a literary genre—somewhat like the detective novel or science fiction. Explanation for the academically challenged: several Apocalypses had been written and some of them could still be found scattered throughout the Bible.

"Apocalypses were written in times of crisis. It was the literature of the downtrodden, of those living in expectation of the Last Judgment, when they would be saved and the wicked punished. That is why, in the Bible, we repeatedly find announcements that the end of the world is at hand—it was a source of hope, a piece of good news. In fact, 'apocaluptein' in Greek means, simply, revelation. Basically, the apocalypse conveys a fairly optimistic view of the world."

From the back of the class, a voice asked if *Mad Max* would belong to the category of apocalyptic works. Laughter. Mr. Bérubé ventured a cautious "if you like." Hope rolled her eyes toward the ceiling. I yawned.

"Can someone identify another apocalyptic story found in the Bible?"

The class was overwhelmed with silence. Mr. Bérubé's eyes swept over the troops.

"Hope, what about you?"

Hope sighed, snapped shut her ballpoint pen and folded her arms.

"The Flood."

"Very good. Excellent! And what can you tell us about the Flood?"

"That it's a suspicious story."

A murmur rippled through the class.

"Suspicious?" asked Mr. Bérubé.

"Yahweh sets in motion the end of the world six pages after having created it. He must have really made a mess of things, wouldn't you say?"

Mr. Bérubé stammered something unintelligible, like a wet "bbl," as though he had just taken a left jab to the stomach. Everyone turned to look at Hope. She disregarded the volley of gazes and remorselessly followed through.

"But what's even more suspicious is that, after drowning the human race like a sackful of kittens, Yahweh promises to never do that again. So can anyone explain why, *even so*, Saint John took the trouble to write the Apocalypse? Evidently the poor man had never read the Old Testament."

The classroom buzzed with whispers. Thrown off balance, Mr. Bérubé got ready to fend off a new series of blows. The bell rang just in time, and we burst out of our seats before he had the chance to expand on the subject.

24. PA RUM PUM PUM PUM

Christmas came upon us with no warning. As usual, my parents invited the Bauermann clan to celebrate Christmas Eve at our house. Come early, bring your own wine.

The aromas of grilled chicken, pickles and doughnuts wafted through the house. The oven had been on since early morning and the main floor felt like a sauna. Thirty or so guests crowded the living room, and Nana Mouskouri's voice floated several decibels above our heads—"Pa rum pum pum pum . . ."

Squeezed between the Christmas tree and the bar, I listened to my cousin drone on about George Michael. High degree of insipidness. Nodding my head mechanically, I killed time by thinking of anagrams of Mikhail Gorbachev. High degree of difficulty.

Amid the hubbub I heard the telephone ring. Jumping at the opportunity, I shot across the living room, just barely avoiding my mother, who was restocking the serving dishes with olives and marinated onions, and picked up the handset just in time. At the other end, Hope's voice sounded strange.

"Are you busy?"

"Absolutely. You're interrupting a crucial conversation on the subject of British pop music."

There was a brief bewildered silence. Hope had not realized that I was joking and I was instantly overtaken by an unpleasant premonition.

"Could you come with me to the police station?"

Red alert. Stretching the telephone cord as far as it would go, I huddled in the staircase that led down to the Bunker, away from prying ears. Halfway down the steps, the air was already three or four degrees cooler.

"What's up?"

"Nothing serious. I just have to go get my mother. Can you borrow the car?"

"I'll be right over."

I hung up, grabbed the keys to the Honda hanging on the wall near the phone and plunged into the coolness of the Bunker. In the time it took to slip on my boots and coat, I was stealing through the back door.

The wind outside was sharp and the ground crunched under my feet. I threaded my way over to the Honda. Fortunately, there were no cars parked behind it (nothing can spoil a covert getaway more than having to ask a sloshed uncle to move his 4x4). I started the car and rolled to the corner of the street before switching on the headlights. With a bit of luck I could make the round trip before anyone noticed my absence. I did not know what to expect, but I knew that I wouldn't want to explain myself later on.

25. MAYHEM AT THE SAINT VINCENT DE PAUL

Hope was waiting for me in front of the Pet Shop, hopping from one foot to the other. She blew on her hands as she sat down beside me. I cranked up the heat and pulled away in the direction of the police station. A minute went by in silence before I dared to ask for details about Mrs. Randall's criminal activities.

"Nothing too terrible. She went to the place where they distribute Christmas food baskets. Know where I'm talking about?"

I knew very well, yes. Every Christmas, the Saint Vincent de Paul Society organized the distribution of non-perishable goods. In fact, my mother had just donated a dozen cans of Campbell's soup and a package of Premium Plus crackers. I hadn't known that Hope and her mother had to rely on food banks . . .

"Of course not, dummy! We've got enough food to last us twenty years! The pantry is crammed and the kitchen cabinets are overflowing. There's even stuff in the bathtub. My mother would rather buy ramen than pay her Hydro-Québec bills!"

"So what was she doing at the Saint Vincent de Paul?"

"The usual obsession: more and more food. And, hey, it's free—just imagine! Like dangling a loaded syringe in front of a junkie."

She gave the door a little punch and let out a growl.

"Anyway, I don't know what happened. She attacked the Christmas tree, broke a couple of things. They called the police."

I remarked that Hope was pretty calm, despite the turn of events.

"Bah, I'm used to it. In Yarmouth, I had to manage things so that the social workers wouldn't send me to a foster home. Someone should give me a degree in the art of negotiation."

I parked the car in front of the police station, just under a sign that said, "Parking Prohibited. Towing At Your

Expense." The street was quiet, with a few snowflakes dancing in the orange light of the mercury arc lamp. All of Rivière-du-Loup was huddled indoors waiting for the Christmas Eve celebrations.

While Hope was having a discussion with the police officer on duty, I pretended to take an interest in the artificial Christmas tree standing in a corner of the waiting room, its branches sagging under layers of tired tinsel. It was easily the saddest evergreen in all of North America.

The officer was lecturing Hope, his fists on the counter. He was not supposed to let a minor take her mother out of jail, whether it was Christmas Eve, Easter morning or two days after Saint-Jean-Baptiste Day. Hope pleaded Mrs. Randall's case: Anyone could see she was not in her normal frame of mind, and the best thing for her would be to go home to rest and to take a generous dose of clozapine and a sedative. A night in prison would do nothing to improve the situation.

The police officer grumbled a little and began to fill out a form. He would make an exception, but only because the detainee had not been violent and had not resisted arrest.

"Do you have a proof of residence?"

With a practised air, Hope produced a telephone bill.

"I'm going to send the file over to the public clinic. Your mother needs to see a health professional."

Hope nodded: Yes, yes, she was familiar with the procedure.

The officer dumped onto the counter Mrs. Randall's personal effects: a handful of change, a wristwatch, a Bic pen (no cap) with multiple teeth marks and a set of keys. While Hope pocketed the items, the police officer opened the cell and escorted Mrs. Randall to the hallway.

Her eyes had a faraway look. Hope's movements were strangely protective as she helped her mother with her coat.

"Are you okay, Mom? How are you feeling?"

"I'm hungry."

"Okay, then, let's go home."

As we drove back, the silence in the Honda weighed ten thousand tons. I steered the car over the icy streets, Hope stared up at the car roof, and her mother, leaning her head against the window and mumbling inarticulately, seemed more preoccupied than ever with the end of days. What new omens had she observed during the last few hours? Graffiti on the wall of her cell? The artificial Christmas tree in the waiting room? The policeman's moustache? Or simply that a girl of seventeen had been obliged to get her mother out of jail on Christmas Eve?

I pulled up in front of the Randall Pet Shop and helped Hope extract her mother from the back seat. Propping her up on either side, we stumbled our way to the door. While Hope fumbled with the lock, Mrs. Randall rambled on, her arm dangling over my shoulder.

Once inside, Mrs. Randall said she was not hungry any more, that she would rather sleep until 1997, or even longer, if possible. That she would wake up only in the event of an unaccredited apocalypse, thank you very much. While Hope removed her boots and coat, I pulled opened the sofa bed. The springs creaked, indicating the need for a few drops of oil. Everything in that dump rusted from the dampness.

Hope helped her mother climb under the sheets, pulled the blankets up to her chin, kissed her on the forehead. Ten seconds later, Mrs. Randall was droning away in Aramaic.

Hope sat down at the foot of the bed and rubbed her eyes. The negotiations with the policeman had demanded an output of thousands of kilowatts in the space of a few minutes. I fidgeted with the car keys and looked around me. The Pet Shop was cold, dark and even messier than usual. An odour of rabbit piss hung in the air. The dining table buckled under piles of paper, notebooks, cash receipts and boxes of Kraft Dinner. I noticed a stack of bills, probably unpaid.

I was embarrassed to be a witness to all this and badly wanted to be somewhere else, and yet I didn't want to turn my back on Hope.

She stopped massaging her eyes and scanned the room. She, too, would have preferred not to be there. I suddenly understood how there might be something reassuring about the end of the world.

Hope sighed.

"Do you know what I dreamt of last night?"

I sat down beside her without speaking. The sofa groaned. Behind us, bits of Hebrew and Akkadian could be heard.

"I dreamt that the animals were coming back to the Pet Shop—giraffes, elephants, zebras. A long line of exotic animals stretching back to Lafontaine Street. They came through the door two at a time and took over. Parrots in the curtains. Lizards in the drawers. Chimpanzees in the closet. They ate our food supplies, but my mother didn't care. She was lying on the couch without any clothes on. I tried to cover her with a coat, but she refused. She laughed and drank wine straight from the bottle, saying that everything was over."

Hope sighed again. She kissed me on the temple.

"Go home. It'll be all right."

Stepping outside, I drew a deep breath of icy air to cleanse my lungs of the smell of the Pet Shop. I brushed my finger over my temple, where Hope had kissed me. All at once, I liked that part of my body.

I got behind the wheel of the Honda and headed home, where my absence had most likely been noticed. Already, I anticipated the barrage of questions. What sort of story could I think up? The car's interior weighed down on me and I switched on the radio. Nana Mouskouri was still pa rum pum pummelling the airwaves.

27. HUNTER-GATHERER

After Christmas, things quieted down. Mrs. Randall regained a modicum of stability thanks to the triple doses of clozapine that Hope meted out to her each morning. At that rate, however, the reserves would probably be depleted by the summer, and no pharmacist would accept a prescription that had been repeatedly crumpled and ironed out. These problems would have to be dealt with in due course.

Since the Christmas episode, I felt I'd been entrusted with new responsibilities. Every day, I made sure that Hope was all right and that her mother had not instigated some new psychodrama. Hope never needed anything but seemed happy to know I was close by.

The end of the winter holidays coincided with the outbreak of the biggest flu epidemic of the decade, a particularly virulent strain concocted in the megalopolises of Southeast Asia. My grandmother swore that this was the Great Return of the Spanish Flu. At school, the classrooms were riddled with unoccupied desks, and everything was running in slow motion. "Carnage" was number one on the word-of-the-week chart.

At the Bauermann residence, my mother's immune system was the first to give way. She found herself bedridden with a temperature of 40, and the slightest movement was enough to make her moan with pain. My father dispatched me to the Steinberg supermarket with a list consisting essentially of large amounts of vitamin C and ground beef. Ultimately, *Homo sapiens* had remained a hunter-gatherer.

I took advantage of the errand to stop by the Pet Shop, since it had been forty-eight hours since I'd last heard from Hope. She hadn't shown up at school or at the Bunker, and she wasn't answering the phone. I had already begun to fear the worst.

As I parked the Honda, there was Hope, who, as it happened, was also on her way to buy groceries. Great minds, etc. She slipped into the front seat.

For someone who was supposed to be down with the flu, she seemed to be in excellent shape. Actually, she had not been sick at all. She had simply been commandeered by her mother, who, without prior notice, had barricaded herself into the pantry by fastening the door with a couple of screws. Quite an unexpected reversal.

"Before shutting herself in, she poured everything that might count as a cleaning product down the toilet: dish soap, detergent, shampoo. She nearly blocked the pipes by trying to flush down the garbage bags."

"What made her do that?"

"Oh, who knows? I have trouble making out what she mumbles through the pantry door. Stuff about germs and the regeneration of the planet. I've given up trying to make sense of it. The upshot is I'm going to take the opportunity to give the apartment a good scrub before I let her out of the dungeon."

"But I thought she was getting better."

"You can't take anything for granted where the Randalls are concerned."

The store was closing in thirty minutes. There were no customers to be seen, only deserted aisles and a long stretch of empty shelves in the Vicks VapoRub section. Clearly, this flu was taking a toll.

We split up to carry out our respective missions. We would rendezvous by the cleaning products in five minutes.

As I went by the refrigerators, I noted the latest Asian invasion: tofu. Out of curiosity, I examined one of the packages. For the time being, this was an exotic and unsavoury item. But in a few years it would be a perfectly ordinary part of our diet, as mundane as Nutella and the H-bomb. In the wake of the Great Tofu War, we would be slightly more Asian, but no one would notice. Another unwritten chapter in the history of the middle class.

My eyes swept over the area as I sought to identify the items that, on the historical level, denoted something new. Which products had appeared since my birth, since my parents' birth? Kiwis, garlic, asparagus? In which year had the first lemons been shipped north of the 47th parallel and sold in our little hinterland town, hundreds of kilometres from the Port of Montreal?

What strange times, when a simple fruit could conjure an enigma.

I loaded up on 50 volts' worth of various citrus fruits—just barely enough to run a quartz watch—and grabbed a package of ground beef without slowing down on my way to the cleaning products aisle. Hope was holding a bottle of detergent in each hand as if gauging which of the two flavours would inflict the most damage. She frowned and dropped both bottles into her cart, where they joined a box of steel wool, some scouring pads, dish soap and a jug of bleach.

Around us, an industrial silence reigned. The only sound was the swishing of the ventilation system. A post-apocalyptic stillness. But what sort of calamity could have left buildings intact, the electricity grid functioning, the products neatly arranged on the shelves?

"Zombie invasion," Hope suggested.

At the far end of the aisle, an obese woman in a fur coat shuffled by, dragging her feet and pushing an empty cart. I had the fleeting conviction that, holy moly, Hope was right: the dead were abandoning the cemeteries!

A moment later there was nothing left but the sound of the fans and a peculiar wistfulness. For a second, Hope and I had been the last people on earth. Now, we were just the last people in the cleaning products aisle.

28. DISTURBING NEWS

Conspicuously located near the cash registers was an enormous bin of marked-down Captain Mofuku ramen— hundreds of astronauts floating in empty space, all wearing the same stupid smile, 3 for 99¢.

Leaning over the bin, Hope very methodically examined the merchandise: (a) she picked up a package of ramen, (b) studied it carefully, (c) made a face, (d) chucked the package into the bin of marked-down candy canes and (e) started over at step (a) apparently with the intention of continuing until she reached the bottom of the container. Should I intervene? The cashier looked on with a jaded expression.

After a while, however, Hope interrupted the inspection and brought to my attention a disturbing piece of news, to say the least. All the packages, without exception, had the same expiry date printed on them: 2001 17 JUL.

29. AMENORRHEA MYSTERIOSA

The list of Eastern perils (influenza, tofu) was soon augmented by a snowstorm originating in the Atlantic basin. The few snowflakes frolicking in the sky around midnight turned into a raging depression that swept over the province, wiping out roads and uprooting hydro towers.

The high school was closed down for the day, and I didn't see Hope until after supper, when she rang at the front door (the door leading directly to the Bunker was now buried under six feet of snow). She was white from head to toe, and her face was completely hidden behind a frost-covered scarf, except for a thin opening for an old pair of ski goggles to peer out of.

When my father opened the door, he yelled something about a mujahideen invasion, which brought a smile to Hope's face. Anything that could boost her morale was welcome.

Clutching mugs of hot chocolate, we huddled under three layers of sleeping bags and took part in Friday-night

Mass: *The Nature of Things*. Suzuki discussed drosophilae and the human genome, but I failed to grasp a single word because of the maddening familiarity with which Hope had draped her leg over mine.

Nothing could be more natural than this simple gesture, but at the same time it was the Halifax explosion, the eruption of Krakatoa, a supernova. I felt more and more dizzy as the warmth of her leg softly radiated through our jeans. If only the blizzard would rage on for another three days!

I glanced at the ground-level window of the Bunker. We were buried far below the surface. On the other side of the glass lay a wall of snow or ash or cement—hard to tell.

During the commercials, Hope related the latest developments on the domestic front. After scrubbing down the apartment, she had extricated her mother from the closet by jimmying the door hinges with a screwdriver. The recluse was not looking very good: hair dishevelled and eyes vacant, she hugged a bag of basmati rice. She had agreed to eat a bowl of soup (quadruple dose of clozapine), refused to take a shower, and then went off to work, anxiously looking around her the whole time. In sum, a partial victory.

The Nature of Things was over and, remote control in hand, I hopped around the channels. Headlining the nightly news was the forecast of a foot of snow by Sunday, and then, as an afterthought, the trial of the captain of the *Exxon Valdez*, the opening of the first McDonald's in Moscow and the arrival of Soviet troops in Azerbaijan. Hope giggled.

"There's a conspiracy of meteorologists to take control of the media!"

On the TV screen images flashed by: a convoy of buses stuck in the snow, cars gone headfirst into the ditch, snowplows, snow blowers, trucks. This was followed by a pathetic variety show, which was then followed by a B movie. Poor Canada.

Lying so close together, we generated a substantial amount of heat, and so Hope removed her woollen sweater. I immediately noticed three band-aids in the crook of her elbow. An odd place to sustain an injury. She admitted, somewhat reluctantly, that she had spent the day at the hospital.

"Oh? Anything the matter?"

"Not really. I had to have some gynecological tests."

While she idly rubbed her leg against mine, she explained that, despite being almost eighteen, she hadn't yet begun to menstruate. She had already consulted a doctor in Yarmouth but had never undergone a serious examination. For the past two weeks she had submitted herself to a battery of tests: blood, lymph, vaginal discharge, urine and other mysterious fluids. She had swallowed barium, had had iodine injections, had been smeared with strange gels, had subjected her pelvis to X-rays and ultrasounds and had even gone through an MRI exam, of which she gave me a description worthy of Steven Spielberg.

I was surprised at having been completely unaware of all those trips to and from the hospital. Hope truly had a talent for camouflage.

"And did they find anything?"

She shook her head.

"The plumbing is in working order. I produce the right hormones and ovulate every twenty-eight days. In fact, my ovaries are more reliable than an atomic clock. The mucous membranes of my uterus refuse to vascularize, but the doctors still don't understand why. They're baffled."

Diagnosis: Hope was afflicted by amenorrhea mysteriosa: "an inexplicable lack of menstruation." In other words, modern gynecology was throwing in the towel. Hope reached toward my cup of hot chocolate, fished out a marshmallow and slipped it into her mouth.

"I've become a medical mystery. Fascinating, isn't it?"

I pictured Hope floating in a jar of formaldehyde—but quickly brushed the image out of my head.

"But, um . . . you're feeling all right?"

"I feel like the Bermuda Triangle."

"What does your mother say?"

"That there's no problem that can't be fixed with a good old end of the world."

30. RANDALL THINKING

I had dozed off in the middle of a documentary on the Guajá, an aboriginal tribe recently discovered in the depths of the Amazonian basin, one of the most secluded regions of the planet. These natives wore loincloths, painted their bodies and had never had any direct contact with post-Columbian civilization. Also, they had greeted the anthropologists' helicopter with a volley of arrows. Good, upstanding people.

The documentary had long given way to an infomercial when the telephone rang. I opened my eyes. The VCR display showed 12:43 a.m. and a bleached-blond motor-mouth was working away on an abdominal exerciser. My hand lifted the receiver and my brain went into gear (in that order).

At the other end, Hope's voice had a sombre ring to it.

"Is it a bad time?"

As a response, I yawned.

"Can you come over to the Pet Shop? I could use a hand."

"You could use a hand? At a quarter to one in the morning?"

"I don't feel like explaining on the phone."

"Okay. I'll be right there."

"Bring some bandages."

"Bandages? Are you hurt?"

She had already hung up.

I listened for signs of activity upstairs. Dead silence. My father had been putting in long days at the cement plant, and I suspected that my mother had been popping sleeping pills for a number of months. The conflict between my brother and father had churned up some choppy water in the vast ocean of her maternal love. Life in a typical North American bungalow.

I got dressed, filled my backpack with whatever might serve from our medicine cabinet—band-aids, gauze, tape, compression bandages with clips—and stole out the back door like a Sioux.

In the street, ice crystals swirled over the pavement. Winter. Endless winter.

Hope was waiting by the door with folded arms and a furrowed brow. I looked her up and down and, seeing no sign of injury, let out a sigh of relief.

Inside the Pet Shop the usual chaos prevailed: dishes and dirty laundry scattered throughout, dust in every corner and a faint odour of reptilian feces. In other words, nothing out of the ordinary, except for Mrs. Randall, who was lying in the middle of the floor unconscious and hastily covered with a shabby bathrobe. Under her head, a bloodstain was soaking into the carpet. Her upper lip—which had probably split when she fell—was still bleeding despite an improvised compress of paper towels. The cleanup would not be easy.

Hope gestured nervously, almost impatiently, in her mother's direction.

"I think she's okay. Aside from the lip, I mean."

"What happened?"

She sighed. After months of denial her mother had finally conceded that errors in calculation were not a factor, and that, to all appearances, there was very little chance of the end of the world coming any time soon.

"So?"

"Use your imagination: You spend twenty years waiting for the end of the world, and poof! Nothing happens."

Despite my best efforts, I couldn't understand. But this was Randall thinking, and there was no point trying to make sense of it.

In any case, Mrs. Randall had decided to (quote) drown her sorrows. Hope explained that in spite of her psychotic inclinations, her mother had always been a diligent young woman, so her aim was not to become *more or less* an alcoholic. She had purchased a bottle of vodka and downed two-thirds of it in thirty minutes flat, wincing as she guzzled.

Then she had removed all her clothes and collapsed in a heap on the floor.

I was worried, so I pressed my forefinger against Ann Randall's wrist. The pulse seemed normal. A little slow, · maybe, but regular.

"Do you think she's in a coma?"

Hope eyed the bottle of vodka with a puzzled expression.

"No. My guess is an adverse reaction between the alcohol and the clozapine."

"Okay, what's the plan?"

"Did you bring the bandages?"

"First we have to disinfect the wound."

"There's some vodka left in the bottle."

She tipped the bottle over a gauze pad and cleaned the wound as best she could. Bits of Sumerian escaped from her mother's lips when she wasn't moaning—an encouraging sign under the circumstances. Already, the bleeding was letting up. Hope placed two enormous bandages over the lip, stating that this would do for now. She would see tomorrow morning whether stitches would be needed.

"Well, we can't just leave her on the floor all night. We have to get her into bed."

Grabbing hold of each end—Hope at her feet and me at her shoulders—we attempted to lift Mrs. Randall. Mission impossible. By virtue of certain mysterious forces, this delicate woman now weighed several tons. There was no way to roll her or push her a little or even raise one of her arms. She was bolted to the carpet.

Finally, we just gave up and, after covering her with some blankets, left her where she was. Hope preferred to watch over her alone and walked me to the door, where she thanked me with a casual kiss on the cheek.

I didn't feel sleepy any more, so instead of going straight home I went for a walk. The truth was I needed to mull over a nagging question: If every Randall became unhinged when the apocalypse failed to show up, was Hope bound to suffer the same fate? The fact that July 17, 2001, seemed infinitely far off did nothing to reassure me.

Lafontaine Street was deserted. Reigning over the window of Elvis Dubé's Karate Studio was a portrait framed in Christmas lights of the King in a kimono. I crossed the street to get away from this spectacle only to find myself in front of Bébé Plus and its display of 1990 models of jogging strollers. The wall was plastered with supersonic infants, the exact antithesis of babies as dead weight.

I thought of the Guajá, those Amazonians who had never had the least contact with modern civilization. They evidently had not missed very much.

The next morning Ann Randall woke up with a gash across her lip and a peculiar glint in her eye.

Since she didn't recognize either her daughter or the Pet Shop, Hope concluded that the vodka was still addling her brain. The amnesia lasted for hours. Ann Randall had apparently ventured out a little farther than what we'd thought—to somewhere in the vicinity of a coma.

The upshot was that we had to provide her with a full rundown of the situation: who we were, where she was, what her job was. By bombarding her with information we managed to reboot the operating system. But instead of simply reverting to normal, the Ann Randall that sprung up before our eyes was completely changed.

Even Hope (who had, after all, seen a lot) was astonished by her mother's new lifestyle. Every morning at seven she would start knocking them back: vodka and orange juice until noon, Bloody Marys for lunch, vodka and soda water until bedtime. And she never left for work without a one-litre thermos of strong tea rectified with rum.

For a beginner, Ann Randall had been quick to find her cruising speed.

But alcohol represented only the first stage in an ambitious strategy. Ann Randall went on to eliminate her legendary program of domestic self-sufficiency in foodstuffs.

Out went the bags of rice, protein supplements and four-litre jugs of water. Frozen food made a triumphant break-through in the Randall fridge: egg rolls, pizza (mini, pocket and traditional), chicken wings, apple turnovers and other edibles brimming with glucose, butylated hydroxytoluene, hydrogenated vegetable oil and Red E123.

And as if this dramatic shift were not enough, Ann Randall started to smoke two packs of Craven "A" per day, not to mention a substantial number of Gauloises (from which she removed the filters), menthol cigarettes and some foul cigarillos laced with port.

She smoked and gorged and imbibed with painstaking fervour, as if she were trying against all odds to set off her own personal apocalypse incrementally. One day at a time.

Hope had stopped administering the clozapine. Not only did the dosage appear to be entirely inappropriate but there was the steadily growing risk of a harmful reac-tion with the alcohol. Having flushed the last pills down the toilet, she kept her fingers crossed.

Ann Randall nevertheless continued to mutter in Sumerian when she slept. Somewhere under the surface, remnants of the young Yarmouth librarian endured.

There were ten minutes left before math class and I walked Hope back to her locker, where she'd forgotten her calculator.

We headed down to the main floor, carried along by the surge of students crowding the stairway. At certain times our feet didn't even touch the ground; we constituted a single carefree mass of hormones and muscles. One false step and we'd be swallowed up and mashed like potatoes.

While we fought for our lives, I asked how Ann Randall was doing. Any better? Hope shrugged—she couldn't really say. More and more she had the impression of living with a stranger, certainly easier to get along with than the previous stranger, but hardly easier to understand.

Actually, Hope was beginning to suspect that the amnesia was long term, as if her mother had deleted large tracts of her memory. Hope had tried to talk to her about Yarmouth, about their frantic departure, but gotten nowhere. And there was no way of determining whether Ann Randall had forgotten or if she simply refused to touch on the subject.

"Maybe she never really knew *why* exactly we left Yarmouth."

"Elementary, my dear Watson. Because we were destined to meet!"

Hope rolled her eyes with a smile of despair.

We arrived at her locker and she began to hunt through the clutter for her calculator. As I watched her digging, I thought of the months of strain she'd been under and marvelled at her ability to keep a cool head at all times. Her mental health was evidently much stronger than her mother's. So, in the end, maybe the Randall family was not completely hopeless.

While I was having these comforting thoughts, I noticed a sort of texture covering the entire inner surface of her locker. At first I supposed it was wallpaper, but it was hardly her style to indulge in frivolous ornamentation.

The strange pattern had actually been written out in felt pen—a skein of hundreds and hundreds of words. But when I looked closer I realized that the words were actually numbers, always exactly the same numbers manically scribbled thousands of times:

17 07 2001 17 07 2001 17 07 2001 17 07 2001 17 07 2001 17 07 2001 17 07 2001 17 07 2001 17

07 2001 17 07 2001 17 07 2001 17 07 2001 17 07 2001 17 07 2001 17 07 2001 17 07 2001 17 07

2001 17 07 2001 17 07 2001 17 07 2001 17 07 2001 17 07 2001 17 07 2001 17 07 2001 17 07 2001

17 07 2001 17 07 2001 17 07 2001 17 07 2001 17 07 2001 17 07 2001 17 07 2001 17 07 2001 17

07 2001 17 07 2001 17 07 2001 17 07 2001 17 07 2001 17 07 2001 17 07 2001 17 07 2001 17 07

2001 17 07 2001 17 07 2001 17 07 2001 17 07 2001 17 07 2001 17 07 2001 17 07 2001 17 07 2001

17 07 2001 17 07 2001 17 07 2001 17 07 2001 17 07 2001 17 07 2001 17 07 2001 17 07 2001 17

07 2001 17 07 2001 17 07 2001 17 07 2001 17 07 2001 17 07 2001 17 07 2001 17 07 2001 17 07

2001 17 07 2001 17 07 2001 17 07 2001 17 07 2001 17 07 2001 17 07 2001 17 07 2001 17 07 2001

33. IN FRIENDLY TERRITORY

Hope and I were getting ready for our final exams, slouched in front of a long commercial for Craftmatic vibrating beds interspersed with bits of B movie, when my mother opened the Bunker door.

"How would you two like to work at the cement plant this summer?"

She explained that the job would involve sorting boxes of documents that had been piling up since the sixties. Eight-week contract, a decent wage, air conditioning. If we would take the trouble to dislodge our adolescent butts from the couch long enough to fill out a few forms, the job was ours.

Hope and I exchanged a quick nod of agreement. My mother tossed me the keys to the Honda, and in no time we were far away.

The sun beamed down, and Rivière-du-Loup smelled of dust and summer vacation. All over town the cherry trees were in bloom, and a snowfall of petals filled the air before being ground down to a beige slurry by the traffic.

On the outskirts of the industrial park, Hope suddenly straightened up in her seat to get a good view of the area. She recognized this place. She had come here about ten months earlier.

She saw herself again, sitting in the tow truck, squeezed between her mother and a giant man smelling of sweat and grease. The Lada, dead from overexertion, followed behind, duly hitched, laden with the vestiges of their previous life: a few articles of clothing, several sacks of rice, a collection of old bibles, cans of beans and tuna in oil, jars of relish and ketchup, and four volumes of *Teach Yourself Russian at Home*. The entire load pressed down on the poor rear shocks and, from time to time, the tailpipe could be heard scraping the asphalt and flinging out a shower of sparks.

Final destination: Élisée Ouellet Valvoline Garage—General Repairs—Iron and Metalwork.

After a heroic 1200-kilometre effort, Comrade Lada ended her days in a muddy yard, amid the remains of hundreds of vehicles. Its carcass was cannibalized for a few months before being reduced to a metal cube. Nothing was as easy to compress as memories.

"Is it still very far?" Hope asked as she turned forward again.

I pointed at the silos and minarets of the cement works. A cement mixer drove past in the opposite direction, and the driver hailed us with a double beep of the horn—he'd recognized the family Honda. I waved in reply. We were in friendly territory.

Mrs. Bilodeau was waiting for us in the office, holding the forms. All we needed to do was to fill in our social insurance numbers, sign at the bottom and keep the pink copy. Between phone calls she talked about the weather and asked us what programs we had enrolled in for the fall term. Her unwavering good mood dipped slightly when Hope asked to be paid in cash. Mrs. Bilodeau answered that normally the accountant never made that kind of exception, but she would see what could be arranged.

She checked our forms, slipped two blank cards into her big Olivetti, rapped out our addresses and filed them in a Rolodex.

"Welcome aboard!"

As we left the office we bumped into my father wearing his white foreman's helmet. He gave Hope a Paul Newman smile and she responded with a wink. They were fond of each other, those two. My father glanced at his watch and asked if Hope would like to visit the facilities.

"There's nothing in the world I'd rather do, Mr. Bauermann."

"Ah! Just seventeen and already a shameless liar!"

He grabbed two old orange hardhats from the back of his 4x4 and cleared away the objects littering the seat: a toolbox, a pair of gloves, a half-empty cup of coffee and a stack of bills held together with a clip—all of it covered with a fine layer of cement.

We sped away, despite the 10 km/h speed-limit signs, and raced toward the first station of the cross.

34. ANYTHING THAT BURNS

As we made our way up the cement route, my father trotted out his little lecture, which I barely listened to, having heard it a hundred times before: The invention of cement went back to the Roman Empire, and it was thanks to the material's exceptional solidity that the structures built back then, like the Baths of Caracalla and the Pantheon in Rome, were still standing. (He would usually add that today half of global cement production took place in the People's Republic of China—a fact that spoke for itself.)

We made a quick stop at the kiln, where my father explained how the raw mix was gradually heated to 1500°C, until it melted and was transformed into clinker, something roughly equivalent to the volcanic rock lining the bottom of barbecues. The clinker was then crushed, the end product being the sacrosanct Portland cement, bedrock of our civilization and pride of the Bauermanns.

I must have dozed off for a few minutes, because all at once the two cohorts were talking granulometry, calcium sulphate ($CaSO_4$) and additives. My father mentioned that sugar was occasionally added to the cement as a way to slow down the setting process, which set Hope off discussing covalent bonds and crystallization. My father was in seventh heaven.

While they chatted about molecular chemistry, a truck passed us, gracefully swung around, and with a belch of diesel exhaust dumped three tons of used tires near the fuel conveyor belt. The tires tumbled over each other like carcasses and, as they bounced, spewed out rainwater and mosquito larvae. Hope looked on wide-eyed.

"You heat the kiln with tires?"

"Tires as well as all manner of automotive detritus—vinyl, plastic, rubber. The plant has an agreement with Élisée Ouellet. We also use residues of solvent, old grease, leftover cuttings of siding. Basically, anything that burns."

We continued on toward the mill and the packing facilities. Hope, suddenly gone quiet, craned her neck to take one more look at the mountain of combustibles at the base of the kiln. The scraps of a civilization that was devouring itself.

Archive duty, Day 1.

Mrs. Bilodeau showed us the place where we would be working, poetically baptized the Filing Cabinet Room. It was a musty, windowless office crammed to the ceiling with about a hundred warped cardboard boxes.

Our mission for the next eight weeks was to sort the contents of the boxes, consisting for the most part of old tax reports, accounting paperwork, press clippings and user's guides for machines now lying ten metres below the surface of the municipal landfill. Some of the documents would be refiled, and some would end up in limbo (i.e., other boxes that other adolescents would open at some improbable point decades in the future). The rest—anything dated before 1981—was to be sent back to the primal void.

Mrs. Bilodeau introduced us to the device that was supposed to dispose of all this paper: an ancient shredder that, despite weighing 50 kilos, was anything but industrial.

"The machine can get quite moody. It can handle about twelve pages at a time, so, above all, don't overload it. If the blades jam, the whole thing has to be taken apart."

I examined the apparatus with a sense of disquiet. Clearly, the odds were that we would spend the better part of our contract managing the appetite of this papyrovore. It would have been much quicker to send our paper trash directly to the kiln's furnace, along with the used tires and the scraps. But I kept this idea to myself. After all, we weren't being paid to sabotage our own source of income.

After a few final instructions—in particular, to watch our fingers—Mrs. Bilodeau let us take over. Hope immediately set the Machine in motion. She picked up a folder titled "Taxes 1968—Annexes" and fed it into the rollers. At the other end, the fiscal year 1968 emerged as curly spaghetti. Hope was exultant.

"I am Shiva, the destroyer of worlds!"

Hope never was at a loss for the appropriate turn of phrase.

36. IN THE BATHS OF ROME

For the rest of the summer, Hope and I filed papers from nine to five. The same monotonous routine was repeated every day: unpack boxes, feed shredder, verify dates, make piles, feed shredder, drink coffee, pack more boxes, feed shredder. The air conditioning was too strong and the coffee too weak, but the pay was good.

Actually, the main drawback of the job was the dust. Everything in the plant generated airborne particles: the crushers, the mills, the conveyors, the chimneys and, especially, the to-and-fro of heavy machinery. The roads were spread with used oil, but a good day of rain was the only thing that could alleviate the problem. It was our bad luck that a dry wind had prevailed over the whole region since June.

We waged a losing battle. Despite the sealed windows and an impressive array of air filters, several kilos of dust seeped into the administrative building every day. At night, the janitor would vacuum the place from top to bottom, but the next morning the slightest surface was once again covered with a whitish film. As resistance was futile, a ban was placed on objects that were impossible to dust off, such as knick-knacks and venetian blinds. There were, however, three exceptions: Mrs. Bilodeau's fern (in constant danger of asphyxiation), computer and calculator keyboards (protected with plastic covers) and human beings (impossible to protect).

As members of the third group, we went home every evening carrying a fine grey powder in our eyebrows, sinuses, pockets, even our underwear. After work, we would go for a dip in the municipal outdoor swimming pool, the only way for us to feel moderately clean again.

We experienced intense moments of joy as the buildings of the industrial park receded in the rear-view mirror. The car radio pumped out a mixed bag of R.E.M., Samantha Fox and the Fine Young Cannibals. In the backyards of the bungalows people lit their hibachis, and hundreds of little plumes of smoke drifted skyward, miniature immolations fuelled by kerosene and pig fat.

The municipal swimming pool was an antiquated, crackled thing built after the war (no one was sure which one), and every spring it faced the threat of permanent closure. The locker rooms reeked of chlorine and damp wood, the showers worked spasmodically, there were gaps in the wall tiles, and the only diving board—a bona fide safety hazard—had been taken down and banished to the couch grass behind a fence.

Swimming in this dilapidated structure afforded me a truly archaeological sort of pleasure. We were the last bathers in the thermae of Rome, just months before the fall of the empire. The barbarians were approaching and we were basking in the sun.

Under her layer of cement, Hope grew more and more tanned, more and more resplendent. Within the entire geometry of the vast universe, there was nothing more graceful than the slender outline of her figure stretched out on a beach towel, the curve of her back or the imprint of her wet foot on the cement. To admire her for a few minutes was all it took for me to descend into profound erotic bliss. But the party in question was oblivious, blinded as she was by the sun and by the end of the world looming and rumbling at the gates of the empire.

Right in the middle of the construction holidays in July, the summer was hijacked by a heat wave. Day after day on the AM radio, Environment Canada repeated the same remorseless information: clear skies, high 32°C, 101.3 kPa pressure on the rise, no wind. The Amazon rainforest.

Sweltering days were followed by stifling nights, and Hope began to suffer from insomnia. There was nothing terribly surprising about this—everyone was having trouble sleeping—but Hope seemed to be more affected than most. She ran on automatic pilot during the day, occasionally conking out or feeding the wrong documents into the shredder. Then, when the sun went down, she grew restless, and by midnight she was completely wired.

For nearly six days she had not slept more than one hour a night, and that hour was fraught with nightmares. There was nothing new on the subconscious front: as always, Hope would see, over and over, processions of exotic animals invading the Pet Shop. Wildebeests in the bathroom, boas in the sink. Zebras, gazelles, zebus.

But, with or without the nightmares, it was impossible to get any sleep at the Pet Shop. Her mother came home from work in the late afternoon, drank and smoked, and then sank like a stone into a deep sleep soaked in gin and nicotine and punctuated with her

Mesopotamian patter. Until 10 p.m. the people using the laundromat could be heard chatting as they sat on the sidewalk, and all night there was the roar of the Chinese restaurant's air conditioning.

The circumstances were in fact so conducive to sleepless nights that Hope just stopped trying. She would steal away from the Pet Shop, wander around for hours or hang out in the bleachers of the municipal stadium. More often than not she would just show up at the Bunker. She would quietly slip in through the back door, which I always left unlocked, and sometimes, when I woke up to take a leak at around 3 a.m., I would find her sitting cross-legged on the couch, blue and spectral in the glow of the cathode screen, totally engrossed by an infomercial.

I would sit down beside her without speaking and watch people rowing in the air, cutting tin cans with a kitchen knife or defrosting steaks, as if this were the most natural event on earth.

38. SPICES AND COLOURING

It was late evening when Hope showed up at the Bunker. She was wearing a grimy T-shirt and smelled of grass and unleaded gasoline. Because, as if the thirty-five hours a week at the cement plant and the morning paper route were not enough, in her spare time Hope mowed the neighbours' lawns in the evenings, after we came back from the swimming pool. If not for the noise, she would have mowed lawns all night. Sleep no longer had any place in Hope Randall's life.

She flopped down across the couch, grabbed the bag of nachos and glanced at the movie I was watching—an old VHS tape of my brother's. The movie featured four survivors aboard a helicopter. Hunkered down on the roof of a shopping mall, they watched as the living dead milled around the parking lot before slowly converging on the doors.

The girl seemed horrified:

"What are they doing? Why do they come here?"

Her companion shrugged.

"Some kind of instinct . . . Memory of what they used to do. This is an important place in their lives . . ."

Two militiamen inspected the roof, armed with M-42s and rifles fitted with telescopic sights—apparently, zombie films were secretly funded by the NRA. Leaning over the skylights, the militiamen scrutinized the interior of the shopping mall. The living dead were rambling past the shuttered stores, among the artificial plants and vending machines.

Hope took off her sneakers, wriggled her toes a little and went to work on the bag of nachos.

"So, what's new?" I asked without taking my eyes off the screen.

"Twenty dollars."

She fished out a wad of oily bills from her back pocket, lifted up one end of a cushion and, as I looked on dumbfounded, slipped her hand into the space under the armrest of the couch, extracting a large brown envelope stuffed with banknotes.

"You keep money hidden inside our couch?!"

"An excellent hiding place, don't you think?"

The envelope was two inches thick. It held Hope's entire savings, representing a year of delivering papers, shovelling snow, pushing lawnmowers and shredding documents at the cement plant. Why hadn't she opened a bank account? No answer. She resealed the envelope and stashed it away again in the couch's entrails.

On the screen, the zombies dragged their feet like sleep-walkers. Growls and blank stares—directing the extras must have been fairly straightforward.

So here was the surprise of the day: Hope, with all her passion for science, just loved zombie movies. The Randall in her, no doubt.

"You know what? I always try to spot familiar faces."

"Sounds like fun. Look, there's our neighbour, Mrs. Sicotte."

"And that's Mr. Bérubé, behind the artificial palm tree."

"Nice one!"

"Hey! There's one who's barefoot!"

Hope was right. At the very edge of the screen, a large living-dead man in a striped shirt was walking around with no shoes or socks. A mere detail, but not for Hope. She was obsessed with shoeless characters.

"What happened to his shoes?"

"No idea."

She moved her toes around in bewilderment. Then she smoothed out the bag of nachos and, grimacing, polished off the pinch of spices and food colouring left at the bottom.

"It reminds me of pictures of Hiroshima after the bombardment. There were barefoot corpses piled up in the streets. As though they'd lost their shoes in the explosion. Weird, eh?"

"They may have been wearing sandals."

"Good point."

39. MARCUS WAS HERE

The sky was saturated with northern lights, a vast turquoise illumination throbbing from the zenith to the horizon in every direction. With a magnetic storm of this magnitude, it would be a miracle if every Hydro-Québec transformer didn't blow before dawn.

The municipal stadium was deserted—not a single living dead to be seen. Yet the baseball field was lit up by a dozen sodium floodlights that probably drained as many megawatt-hours as Equatorial Guinea.

A brand-new sign had been nailed up near the ticket booth:

SUMMER HOURS

NO AXESS

AFTER 11 P.M.

We went in without bothering about the sign or the hour.

From a plastic bag that she had brought along Hope pulled out a Mason jar half-filled with a clear liquid.

"Vodka," she explained.

She regularly drew off some of the contents of her mother's bottles, which she then cut with water (no holds were barred when it came to reducing maternal blood alcohol levels). But on that night, instead of pouring the vodka down the toilet, Hope had decided to hold a tasting session.

"Purely out of scientific curiosity. I'd like to know what goes on inside Ann Randall's skull."

She unscrewed the lid and took a swig with her nose scrunched up. All for a good cause. She handed me the jar, which I raised to the health of Marie Curie before helping myself to a large gulp—grmmppphlltz!!

The night's dew had soaked the bleachers, so we opted for the greasy bench in the dugout. We took turns drinking from the jar at a leisurely pace while we read the graffiti carved into the plywood: "Marcus was here," "Die Scum" and "Go hang yourself."

Using her set of keys, Hope added "17 07 2001." Sigh.

I found a bat that had rolled under the bench, so between gulps we swatted pebbles into the stratosphere. The only thing that could be heard on the field was our conversation punctuated with the clack of the wood striking the stones.

The vodka started to abrade the rough edges of reality. Hope held forth on Mikhail Gorbachev's first name, Jewish folklore and the end of the Cold War. She sent a pebble flying into centre field and reclaimed the Mason jar, which by now held only a few drops of vodka.

Appearing out of nowhere, a cat loped across the field. When it caught sight of Hope, it swerved around and came over to rub against her ankles for a moment. Then it suddenly took off again to resume its feline business.

"Hey—my mother's had some news from the Randall family."

"Really?"

"My cousin Dan went berserk at the beginning of the month."

"When was he expecting the world to end?"

"March. Theoretically, the planet was supposed to get sucked into a black hole."

To emphasize how mistaken her cousin was, she pointed to the stadium with a sweeping gesture and capped her mute commentary with a shot of vodka—the last.

"He shut himself in his cellar with a crate of dynamite and sent the bungalow into orbit."

"No kidding?"

"My mother received the clipping from the *Chronicle-Herald*, if you don't believe me. There's even a picture of the crater. A nice big hole that's probably still smoking as we speak."

The Randall family was always full of surprises, most of them not very good. There was an awkward silence while I tried to calculate the time remaining before July 17, 2001. Hope read my mind.

"Don't worry. There are still 3,984 days left."

Very comforting.

Hope had stepped up to the plate with the bat resting on her shoulder, ready to send a perfect pebble flying over Greenland, when the floodlights suddenly went out. As our eyes gradually grew accustomed to the dark, the turquoise throb of the northern lights reclaimed possession of the sky.

Hope sighed.

"There is a time to gather stones together and a time to cast stones away."

In conclusion, the effects of vodka were the following: Bolshevik breath, slurred speech and cryptic statements. As for learning exactly what was cooking inside Ann Randall's head, we still had no idea. The experiment was a failure—so much for basic research.

40. TELEVISION IS THE ENEMY

One morning in August, without warning, Ann Randall chucked her miserable job and announced that she had resolved to start her life over again in the Dominican Republic. She was going to be a barmaid in a hotel on the Caribbean seashore. Sun, palm trees, coral beaches and rum.

"It's time I rounded out my education," she declared as she poured a measure of Moskovskaya into her orange juice.

Seeing that her daughter was unconvinced, Ann Randall produced the application for employment at the Club Playa de Puerto Plata, including the duly completed forms, the stamped envelopes and two passports sent away for early in the summer under the pretense of needing them for an unspecified vacation. There could be no doubt: she had embarked on a career of alcoholism with the efficiency of a model student.

Incredulous, Hope examined her brand-new passport. A grown-up discussion was called for. She made it clear that she would not let herself be dragged along to the Third World. That she would soon be entering junior college. That in a few months she would legally be an adult. That she had absolutely no intention of being Lada'd a second time. That she had plans of her own, which happened to be incompatible with the Dominican Republic and piña coladas. That, that and that.

Her mother looked at the passports, grumbling a little, but willing to give some ground. So she began immediately to search through the Yellow Pages for a local watering hole.

Our summer contract at the cement plant had just ended and we had, without missing a beat, resumed our daily TV marathon: hours upon hours of watching the news, *The Price Is Right*, *Three's Company* and all the memorable trash that, as Hope put it, made up "an enlightening snapshot of North American civilization on the eve of its annihilation." Whoopee.

Meanwhile, my own mother was overpowered by a peculiar attack of orientalism. She'd started cooking with tofu, studied guidebooks to Zen meditation, bought Buddhas and bonsais at Zellers. What's more, she plonked

one of those pint-sized evergreens on the TV set as a dec-
laration of war against popular Western culture. Television
was the Enemy.

The bonsai turned out to be an insufficient argu-
ment, so, without even reading the riot act, my mother
ousted us from the Bunker, right in the middle of a
James Bond festival. We would have to catch *Moonraker*
some other time.

Brutally forced to go cold turkey, we wandered the
streets looking for a substitute—any screen would do.
The Princess Theatre was closed for the week (due to
"flooding," according to the sign taped to the door, but
we assumed this meant the plumbing). Hope looked over
the fall program of the Great Explorers and appeared
mildly interested in the visit of Katia Krafft, scheduled for
late November. But could we survive until then in the
absence of televised stimulation?

The sun was setting, and Hope suggested we go to the
drive-in theatre. Unfortunately, the only drive-in in the
area had closed down years ago, and since then the screen
had been used for target practice by men at loose ends
who, on Friday nights, would come down to empty their
.22s and drink lukewarm Black Label beer. It was a destination best avoided.

Hope sighed and kicked at a steel bolt, which in turn
put a star-shaped ding in the door of a big, brand-new

Ford. She asked me if I thought my mother's TV embargo would be maintained for much longer.

"Until I go to university, I guess. When she's made her mind up about something, she sticks to her guns."

(Which, come to think of it, reminded me of someone else I knew.)

In our boredom, we watched the mercury arc street-lamps light up one by one along Lafontaine Street. The notice in the window of the funeral co-op announced a wake for Mrs. Louis-Robert Gendron-Lavallée, who had passed away on the night of July 13. In lieu of flowers, donations may be made to the Canadian Cancer Society.

At times the apocalypse seemed very near. At other times, it seemed far, far away.

41. THE OPHIR III

Having squeezed the tent, sleeping bags and cooler into the trunk of the Honda, we fled the city like a couple of neo-hippies, with the windows down and our hair blowing in the wind.

We headed randomly eastward. At Cacouna, we tried our luck on a tractor road that snaked through black spruce until it reached a rocky cove. The place was deserted, sunny and reeked of kelp. Adopted unanimously.

We spent a languid afternoon reading in the sun. The wind drove away the occasional mosquito, and the beer waited in the cooler for nightfall. Suntan lotion and hot dogs cooked over hot coals—the camping trip was a veritable anthology of the maudlin clichés that make life bearable. Yes, with the city far behind and the Cold War receding to a distant horizon, life all at once seemed oh so bearable.

While she stirred the embers with a twig, Hope brought me up to date on her mother, who had succeeded (believe it or not) in getting hired at a bar without so much as an interview. Hope asked me if I knew the place. It was called the Ophir.

"You mean the Ophir *III*," I specified. Of course I knew it. It was legendary in Rivière-du-Loup.

The very first Ophir was a hotel built during the boom generated by the Grand Trunk. It looked like a gold-rush brothel: a white four-storey building, all wood and banisters, set on the side of a hill. However, this historic building burned down in sketchy circumstances at the end of the 1960s and was immediately replaced by the Ophir II, Serving Canadian and Polynesian Food. This second avatar also went up in smoke as a result of an unfortunate deep-fryer mishap. Since then, the renowned street corner has been occupied by the Ophir III. Bar Salon Fireproof—*Bienvenue aux Dames*.

Of course, the surrounding neighbourhood had not retained very much of its heritage charm. The Grand Trunk trains, hauled by locomotives spewing fire and steam, had given way to liquid nitrogen tank cars and to containers—Maersk, Hanjin, Hapag-Lloyd and China Shipping.

"Interesting story," Hope said.

She pulled her twig out of the fire and examined its glowing tip.

"My mother decided to work at the Ophir because of the name. Did you know it comes from the Bible?"

"Really?"

"Ophir was the mythic land of King Solomon's gold mines. My mother saw it as a good omen."

She planted the tip of the twig in the sand, but then lost interest and threw it in the fire. The thought of her mother working in a bar was obviously upsetting her. I reassured her that her mother could have done worse than the Ophir.

"I guess," Hope sighed.

She admitted that, in fact, her mother seemed to have found a greater degree of balance and serenity than ever before. The Ophir was having a better effect than the clozapine, largely because the bottles were not equipped with measured pourers and the inventory was managed with good-natured laxness. A point in favour of cocktail bars. Ann Randall was now indulging all day long and worshipped the resident barflies as true Doctors of Alcohology. In the field of quiet self-destruction, she had found her masters, and she was constantly bending Hope's ear about the coterie of regulars sitting at the counter.

"You'd be surprised to see how much those men can teach us!"

Hope rolled her eyes. "To listen to her you'd think that the Dalai Lamas go to the Ophir when they retire!"

I made a mental note of this information. It would be good to know where to look if ever we needed a Dalai Lama.

42. BANISHED FROM EDEN

The sun went down in an endless sky. The nearest cloud was little more than a microscopic orange dot directly over Baffin Island, and we decided to sleep under the stars. Having grafted our sleeping bags together, we spooned on the coarse sand ten paces from the fire.

I woke up in the middle of the night. Hope was fast asleep—the wind blowing in from the open water had cured her insomnia. I could hear the faint wash of the ebb tide, and at the far end of the mud flats, if I raised my head a little, I could see the reassuring pulse of the lighthouse at Cap de la Tête au Chien: one long flash followed by two short ones. Overhead, the constellations had travelled quite a distance, so that Orion now looked down on the river.

For a long while I gazed at the Milky Way, trying to see it for what it was: our galaxy's downtown. According to Hope, the Earth orbited somewhere in the suburbs, in an insignificant galactic arm. It was enough to make you feel irrevocably confined to the margins.

The feeling was disturbing but not unpleasant. Hope and I were alone not just on the planet but in this whole sector of the universe. Adam and Eve, banished from Eden, exiled on a virgin planet that stank of kelp.

43. DETAILS ON PAGE 47

We re-entered civilization the next morning, our clothes full of sand and our hair full of smoke. Hope's hand rested on my thigh, and I kept having an urge to drive all the way to Japan, but reality intervened and we had to stop to fill up the tank.

I spotted an old mom-and-pop gas station on the 132. The pumps were a sixties vintage, and a yellowing sign announced just one item: *régulier 43.8¢/litre avec service*. The attendant, a sort of sumo wrestler wearing a John Deere cap, was sitting in the sun on a pyramid of cans of motor oil, reading the newspaper. The Honda rolled over the compressed air hose, triggering the bell, and the wrestler stood up unhurriedly with the tabloid folded under his arm. As he pressed his hands against the edge of my window, I felt the car listing.

"Ahoy, captain! What's your pleasure?"

"Fill it up, please."

"Right you are."

He laid the newspaper on the roof of the car and set to work. Hope stepped out into the sun. I watched her stretch. As she raised her arms her T-shirt lifted slightly and exposed her navel. There was a mahogany glow on the perfectly tanned surface of her belly, a stirring testimony to the many hours spent at the municipal swimming pool since June.

She winked at the attendant, and in response he touched two fingers to the visor of his cap. By way of making contact with the world again, she picked up the newspaper roasting on the roof the car. A moment later she leaned over toward me.

"Have you seen this?"

I skimmed the first page and raised my eyebrows. I could see nothing very significant—just the results of the Formula 1 Grand Prix in Montreal.

"No, in the corner!"

I looked. Set in a small box between the weather and the winning Mini-Loto numbers was an item announcing the Iraqi invasion of Kuwait and the ensuing wrath of the Most Holy United States of America, whose craving for petroleum was unquenchable. A prelude to all the nastiness to come. Details on page 47.

So much for our return to civilization.

44. SATELLITE TV

The sweltering summer was followed by a rainy fall. The wind slapped dead leaves and plastic bags against the windows of the Bunker, which was once again submerged in semidarkness.

A new era, a new routine. We had started junior college, and Hope was still plagued by insomnia. The fall slipped past like a 16 mm film that has been wound and rewound on the projector until it ends up flapping around in the air.

Toward the end of November, my mother's TV embargo suffered a major setback. Robert, the owner of the Ophir III, had a three-metre parabolic antenna installed on the roof of his establishment. The appendage was clearly too heavy for the frail roof structure, and its installation immediately gave rise to non-stop conjecture as to the exact moment the 300 kilos of galvanized steel would plunge through the layers of asphalt shingles, wood, mineral wool and drywall and crash down in the middle of the counter, right at a spot where the Dalai Lamas (who proved to be skilled geometers) had incidentally stopped sitting.

Robert had kind-heartedly promised everyone drinks on the house in the event of such a disaster.

Hope and I had front-row seats for the antenna's inauguration. But we were out of luck, because all the contraption could pull in was snow, U.S. evangelists and the Albuquerque weather report ("sunny, 78°F, sun rising at 6:34"). Only subscribers could unscramble the interesting channels, and subscriptions were restricted to citizens of the American Empire.

Yet Robert was a man of honour, and the solution to this problem arrived in the mail two weeks later in a bubble-wrap envelope adorned with lovely tropical stamps and a return address in Nassau, Bahamas. Inside the envelope was a pirate decoder (Robert preferred the term "homemade"), including a keyboard on which, once a week, the user had to enter a password obtained through a highly democratic subscription. Hurray for free enterprise!

Now the big saucer could pick up 150 television channels, but of these the screen yielded nothing but the Sports Network, for the entertainment of our Dalai Lamas. On behalf of the rising generation, Hope and I laid claim to the slightest program break. However, program breaks were a rare thing indeed (you could always find a baseball game being played somewhere on the globe), so in total we managed to watch about 45 minutes of TV a day, in bits and pieces. We very sensibly sacrificed *Gilligan's Island* in order to optimize our use of airtime—which essentially involved staying abreast of preparations for the huge, impending mess in the Fertile Crescent.

Since no journalist had as yet been deployed, we had to bide our time watching stock footage. UN headquarters. Marines polishing their assault rifles. F-14s taking off from American aircraft carriers. Iraqi or Iranian or Jordanian military personnel driving jeeps across the desert. Forests of oil derricks.

On CNN, political pundits sounded off on the subject of Saddam Hussein. One of them—possibly affected by the recent death of Curtis LeMay—pounded the table, asserting that if the Iraqi army refused to lay down its arms, the U.S. Air Force ought to roll out its ballistic missiles and blast that horde of barbarians back to the Stone Age.

And so on.

The weeks passed with flurries of activity and snow. We celebrated Hope's eighteenth birthday, then Christmas. For the first time in years my parents abstained from hosting the Bauermann powwow, and Christmas Eve was observed with a reduced contingent. Hope was the only one who was not a family member, and my father fell over himself to make her feel at home. He had even given her

David Suzuki's latest book as a gift. How in the world had he learned of her admiration for the famous biologist? No clue.

Hope was radiant. And why not? Her mother, pleasantly soused behind the counter of the Ophir III, was celebrating under the protective gaze of a dozen Dalai Lamas. No one mentioned it, but we thought back to her incarceration a year before, which already seemed centuries ago. So we lightheartedly raised a glass of Baby Duck to the future.

Three weeks later Baghdad was pounded by the first wave of Tomahawk missiles.

45. THE BEGINNING OF THE WORLD

A fine snow was falling on the neighbourhood where the train station was located, and a convoy of containers stirred up graceful powdery swirls as it trundled along the tracks.

We shook the snow from our boots and coats, swung open the door and entered the close atmosphere of the Ophir. Seaport taverns must have given off that same odour of fermented barley and tobacco back in the glory days of buccaneering. It was a stench that contained more history than any museum.

A quiet half-light filled the room. It was nearly empty, except for three Dalai Lamas working the first booze shift at the bar. A surrealist match of buzkashi was under way on the TV screen: some horsemen were dragging a veal carcass through the dust on an unnamed mountain range of Central Asia. SportsChannel had evidently diversified its programming.

Ann Randall, inconspicuously tipsy, stared into space with a cigarette hanging at the corner of her mouth. She greeted us with a thin smile and leaned over the counter to kiss us on the cheeks.

"Hi, you two! How're you doing?"

"Couldn't be better. Is the TV available?"

She silently consulted the Dalai Lamas, who responded by casting an indifferent glance at the game of buzkashi (3–0 for the Uzbek team). No objections, as long as we freed up the airwaves for *Hockey Night in Canada*.

Hope immediately tuned in to CNN, where the latest pictures from Iraq confirmed our worst predictions: the Americans seemed determined to wipe Baghdad off the face of the planet.

Norman Schwarzkopf stated at a press conference that the American armed forces were in fact carrying out delicate surgical operations. It was now possible to "neutralize" a high-ranking Iraqi official as he ate breakfast, while his wife continued to munch on her Al-Mecca

Flakes at the other end of the table. At worst, there would be a few grains of plaster to be brushed away from the sleeve of her dressing gown. Ballistic lacework.

Ann Randall served us two glasses of Baghdad Sunrise, a drink invented by Hope: a double shot of instant coffee, Moskovskaya, Jack Daniel's and a drop of cream. Ideal fuel for keeping the troops alert and lively until closing time. Because that was how long we needed to wait to reclaim possession of the television for an hour or so, the time it took to evict the Dalai Lamas, mop the floors, roll the small change and flip the bar stools up onto the counter. But what wouldn't we do in exchange for our daily dose of TV—and at any hour, too, since there was always something going on in Baghdad. The American media, shrewdly embedded within the armed forces, broadcasted the fireworks live, night and day.

Hope dubbed it "Glasnost, Texas-style."

We spent the evening in our usual spot. Hope reviewed her notes for Integral Calculus 101, while I slapped together a Spanish composition, and between periods of the hockey game we watched the methodical destruction of the ancient city of the Abbasid caliphs. For our supper, we had packed a supply of astronaut-flavoured ramen, every package stamped with the fateful date.

Toward midnight there was hardly a soul left in the bar. Everyone had cleared out after the Canadiens' defeat, which happened to coincide with the end of the Sports Fans' Special: 2 for 1 on all Labatt products—enough to sway even the most avid athlete. Therefore, hardly a soul left, except for a CNR brakeman marking the end of his shift before heading over to the company hotel to snore the night away. Hope took advantage of the situation to regain control of the television.

The sun was rising over the Iraqi desert, and CNN was airing its nightly hit parade: a salvo of Tomahawk missiles had (delicately) struck a residential neighbourhood during the night. Captured through a zoom lens, the explosions resembled molten balls of silica. A mad glassblower was running amok in Baghdad, with his blowpipe glowing white-hot.

The brakeman stopped poking around in the peanut bowl and stared at the screen.

"Looks like the end of the world," he sniffed.

"Or the beginning of a new one," Hope replied glumly.

The man gave her a bewildered look before focusing his whole attention back on the peanut bowl. I wondered whether we hadn't been better off before the satellite antenna went into operation.

Just as we were about to set out for the Ophir for another night of fragmented TV, I received a call from Norbert, a classmate in my drama course, who informed me that they were "cracking open a few cold ones" at his place in order to fend off the ambient gloom.

Hope said she was in, so we instantly changed the flight plan. After a stopover at the corner Irving station to pick up a case of beer, we landed at Norbert's. The door was opened by a glassy-eyed individual with a goatee, an Afro haircut and a black cat perched on his shoulder. He invited us to leave our boots in the hallway and slipped away, reeling.

It could be roughly estimated that Operation Cold Ones had been in full swing since mid-afternoon. Twenty-odd partiers filled the living room and a dozen others were scattered around the apartment. No sign of Norbert on the radar screen. Clusters of empty bottles surrounded virgin canvases, tubes of paint and bundles of brushes marinating in solvent. R.E.M. was playing at full blast, and off in a corner, clips of Kuwait flashed by on a black-and-white TV that no one was watching.

An aroma of hash and Hawaiian pizza wafted through the shambles. I wondered if there was any pizza left.

Hope wanted to hang out in the kitchen, at a reasonable distance from the musical epicentre. On our way there we bumped into plaster casts, two-by-fours and headless mannequins. As we passed the washroom, behind the shower curtain I could make out the silhouette of what I believed was a mannequin topped with a deer's head. A dozen wet towels covered the floor, and perched on the toilet tank was an impressive collection of mouldy old Marvel comics—dozens of issues of *Captain America*, *Spider-Man* and *Fantastic Four* left there for the literary enjoyment of visitors to the lavatory. The pile, which reached almost to the ceiling, sagged sideways and was just barely prevented from collapsing by the corner of the wall.

In the kitchen, several blackened butter knives were arranged in a star shape around one of the stove burners. Cases of beer had been stacked on the window ledge, and the window itself was covered with a good half-inch of frost. Sitting on either side of a litter box, two bearded guys were listing all the films since the fifties that featured the destruction of the Statue of Liberty. They seemed to be taking the discussion very seriously.

Hope, who was famished, raided the fridge. We sat on the counter with our two beers and a jar of Polish-style pickles. The smell of dill and vinegar blended harmoniously with the fragrance of cannabis resin. Equipped with a relatively clean fork, Hope speared a pickle.

"Who lives here?"

"Norbert Vong."

"Norbert *Vong*? That's not very 'local colour.'"

"He's from Laos."

While I wrestled with the pickles, Hope spied a bottle of nail polish on the edge of the sink and carefully examined the label.

"Is his name really Norbert?"

"I think he changed his first name when his family came to Quebec. They immigrated in the late seventies."

"Boat people?"

"Exactly. If I'm not mistaken there were six or seven Laotian families who settled in Rivière-du-Loup."

"A strange place to immigrate."

"You know, now that you mention it, they all left for Toronto after two years. The Vongs are the only ones who stayed."

Hope opened the bottle of nail polish and sniffed at the contents inquisitively. Then she daubed some polish on her thumbnail, which turned an unlikely electric blue flecked with sparkles. If I'd been asked to come up with a name for that colour, I would have leaned toward Plutonium.

Finding the results to her liking, Hope went on to do the all the nails of her left hand, followed by those of her right hand. While waiting for the solvents to dry, she dreamily chomped on a pickle. The hash fumes were unleashing swarms of neurotransmitters in our brains.

"Can I steal a cigarette from someone?"

Three hands instantly proffered three packs. She lit a Craven "A," took a deep puff, and exhaled. Hope smoking a cigarette—I couldn't believe my eyes.

"Scientific curiosity, my dear Watson!"

She pulled off her socks (thick grey woollen ones that she bought by the dozen at the army surplus), sent them sailing to the far side of the kitchen and began to paint her toenails. I felt as if I were observing an extremely rare natural phenomenon, like a total eclipse of the sun, or the flowering of a bamboo forest, or the eruption of Mount St. Helens.

"I have to go pee," she announced as she completed the final brush stroke. "We'll be right back after the break."

She disappeared, waving her fingers in the air. Left alone, I fondly observed her socks on the floor. It was the first time I ever felt moved by an old pair of woollen socks.

Near the litter box, one of the bearded guys (the one wearing engineer-style glasses) was explaining that American filmmakers had proven incapable of destroying New York and always ended up attacking symbols—the Statue of Liberty or the Empire State Building, for example—instead of *real* buildings.

" . . . and that's because the Americans have never been attacked on their own territory. New York has never been bombed or napalmed. They haven't experienced destruction on the tangible, architectural level. Any Lebanese man on the street knows more about it than all the specialists in Hollywood put together."

As he spoke, he reached over to the case of beer and exchanged an empty bottle for a full one.

"When a Japanese director decides to raze Tokyo, it's a whole other kettle of fish. They're very thorough. You can sense the expertise. Have you seen *Akira*?"

His listener shook his head. The guy wearing glasses took a swig of beer.

"The Japanese, my friend, really know what they're doing."

I was wondering whether this theory made any sense or if, on the contrary, it came under the heading of unadulterated crap, when Hope suddenly re-entered my field of vision. Standing in the kitchen doorway, nails sparkling and eyes aghast, she looked stunned. She was holding an old issue of *Spider-Man* stained with dampness and obviously drawn from the stack on the toilet tank. It was opened to a page full of ads.

"Have you seen this?"

I arched my eyebrows. All I could see was that good old advertisement for Amazing X-Rays, and I thought Hope must be joking around. She shook her head.

"No, in the corner!"

My eyes shifted to the left and my heart froze.

PREPARE YOURSELF!

THE WORLD WILL END ON JULY 17, 2001

DON'T WAIT TO DISCOVER

THE PROPHECIES OF CHARLES SMITH

TRANSLATED INTO 18 LANGUAGES (INCLUDING TIBETAN)

SEND MAIL ORDERS TO:

LEVY PUBLISHING — PO BOX 2816362 NEW YORK

47. A TINY OASIS OF WARMTH

I read and reread the box in disbelief, repeating that it was nothing more than a coincidence, but Hope wasn't buying that. For her, the probability of another crackpot predicting the end of the world for July 17, 2001, was on the order of 1 in 16 billion.

Having suddenly lost our appetite for partying, we spent a long time searching for our boots in the jumble of soles, laces and odours of the apartment hallway. Hope ended up putting on a pair at random (surreal white Tony Lama boots).

The city was dead—not a single car in the streets. A warm front had rolled in during the evening and we could hear the snow crackling on the ground. We were (once again) the last living creatures on the continent, surrounded by thousands of abandoned bungalows where the lights went on every night and went off every morning, activated by an army of automatic timers.

We walked slowly. More tired than she had let on, Hope clung to my waist and leaned her head on my shoulder. I heard her grumble as we passed the municipal stadium.

"Charles Smith. Talk about a name for a prophet."

It was colder inside the Bunker than outside. We climbed under the covers without even undressing.

Hope fell asleep almost at once, pressed against my back, her breasts resting between my shoulder blades. I sensed an erection taking shape under the layers of bedding but refrained from making the slightest movement. I was afraid to interfere with an infinitely delicate ceremony: Hope's breath on my neck, her arm across my chest, the tips of her fingers under my belt.

Our two bodies formed a tiny oasis of warmth in a universe that had been cooling down inexorably for fifteen billion years.

48. CRUMBS AND FOAM RUBBER

I woke up in the early afternoon, my head throbbing and my heart tilting at a forty-five-degree angle. The other half of the bed was empty and cold. Hope had decamped to take care—I assumed—of Hope's business.

I swallowed three pills of the first analgesic I could find, took a boiling-hot shower and went upstairs. The house was deserted and gave me the impression of a third-rate New Zealand sci-fi movie. The light hurt my eyes. I hated Sundays. I poured myself a large glass of orange juice, snapped up the newspaper (with a flurry of toast crumbs) and went back down to the Bunker.

I was about to drop down on the couch when a detail caught my attention: one of the cushions had been removed and then put back askew. A bad feeling came over me.

I tossed the cushion aside, plunged my arm inside the couch and groped around in its entrails for a good while. There could be no mistake: instead of a thick envelope stuffed with money, my hand found nothing but springs, foam rubber and unidentified crumbs.

Hope had closed her secret account.

49. THE END IS NIGH

Hope got off the bus and, without any hesitation, strode across the terminus, her Tony Lamas cutting white streaks through the grey of the morning.

She stopped at the foreign exchange office to transmogrify a few dollars and used the change to buy a map of Manhattan. Then she went to a pay phone and dialed 411 to get the address of Levy Publishing, which she memorized. According to the map the Lower East Side was an hour's walk away.

Hope was in no rush.

She headed due south on Broadway in the light rain, moving at a relaxed pace, taking everything in with her curious eyes. Each stride brought something new to marvel at. At the corner of Lafayette, she gave a dollar to a vagrant carrying a sign that read The End Is Nigh. In the window of a Dairy Queen, she waved to a double of David Bowie sipping a milkshake cold and long. From time to time she would stop to tap on a wall and was amazed to find it dense and solid against the palm of her hand. So this is what New York looked like, the city so often attacked by Hollywood.

As she passed a TV repair shop she remembered—oddly enough—the existence of a certain Mickey, several hundred kilometres to the north, and ducked into a telephone booth to bring him up to date, calling collect.

MICKEY: What the hell are you doing in New York?

HOPE: I want to meet Charles Smith.

MICKEY: The prophet? Have you got his address?

HOPE: No.

MICKEY: You have a plan?

HOPE: I'm going see his publisher to start with. After that, I'll see how things stand.

MICKEY: It makes no sense.

HOPE: . . .

MICKEY: Okay. Fine. *Assuming* the publisher agrees to give you the address. Do you really think this Smith, how can I put this . . .

HOPE: . . . will turn out to be a more reliable source of information than a package of ramen?

MICKEY: You took the words right out of my mouth.

Momentary silence.

HOPE: We'll see.

Hope stepped into the lobby of one of those glazed-brick office buildings so prevalent on the Lower East Side. She ran her finger over the list of tenants: an import-export company, a photography agency, a number of unidentified businesses and (bingo!) the offices of Levy Publishing, suite 701.

While the freight elevator, of Great Depression vintage, climbed from floor to floor in painfully slow motion, Hope tried to work out a clever plan of attack. She had not come up with anything by the time the gate opened onto the seventh floor. She would have to ad lib.

The offices of Levy Publishing sat directly opposite the elevator, behind a glass door that Hope walked through without hesitating.

There was no one at the reception desk. Through a side door, Hope glimpsed some girls who were busy filling cardboard boxes with piles of books. Seeing that the girls took no notice of her, Hope used the time to survey the reception area. A few chairs, a desk, a corridor and—notably—a large portrait of Charles Smith, a man in a white medieval-style shirt, with piercing eyes and a pair of eyebrows worthy of Zeus.

The picture covered one whole section of wall, an indication of Smith's stature in the Levy Publishing catalogue.

"May I help you?"

Hope turned and found herself standing face to face with a generic receptionist: fifty-sevenish, grey pantsuit, hair tied up in a bun, an air of endless weariness and endless impatience.

"I'm looking for Mr. Smith."

"You're looking for Mr. Smith?" the secretary responded, narrowing her eyes.

Hope gave her an emphatic nod, thinking it better not to say any more. The secretary picked up the telephone and exchanged a few words with an unspecified individual while looking Hope up and down. Her gaze lingered momentarily over the plutonium-blue nail polish and the cowboy boots, which elicited a nascent smile. Then she hung up.

"Please come this way."

She walked down the corridor ahead of Hope. The place had seen better days: pitted walls, stained carpet, swarms of dust mites. To all appearances, Levy Publishing was not in the habit of hosting formal visits.

At the far end of the hall, behind the very last door, was a man in shirtsleeves with a yarmulke riding askew on the top of his skull. Seated at a huge oak desk, he was eating a Reuben on rye over a paper plate. A little plaque on the desk identified him as Sammy Levy *himself*, the founder-owner-director of Levy Publishing and the most unpleasant publisher in the known universe.

In a corner of the office, a TV on mute was tuned to CNN: George Bush giving a press conference with the stock prices streaming by at the bottom of the screen. A subtle dialogue going on between the two.

The room was spare, but the window afforded a breath-taking view of New York. Dozens of skyscrapers filled the field of vision, and at the mouth of the Hudson, to the west, rose the twin towers of the World Trade Center. A commercial space like this in Manhattan must have cost a fortune, but, given the condition it was in, Hope figured that the lease had been signed in the 1970s.

Levy never took his eyes off his corned beef sandwich except to glance up at CNN. He did not seem very inclined to have his meal interrupted, and Hope wondered whether she should wait or press ahead. After a minute, Levy licked his fingers, straightened up in his chair and deigned to look at her.

"Nice boots."

"Thank you."

"So you're looking for Charles Smith?"

She nodded.

"I have no idea where he is."

In response to Hope's evident astonishment, Levy explained that Levy Publishing was just a run-of-the-mill publisher with no control over the physical existence of Charles Smith. As it happened, said Charles Smith had been unreachable for two or three years, which, from a strictly administrative point of view, was not a problem, as he had ceded all rights to his book against a lump sum. The guy may as well have been dead for all the difference it would make.

"Might even increase sales," Levy mumbled.

Hope could not believe it. How could you lose touch with a prophet? Levy burst out laughing. He apparently found the word *prophet* quite amusing. Charles Smith, he said, was no more than a trademark. A product. There was a market for everything and the apocalypse represented a rapidly expanding niche.

"Any other questions?"

Hope muttered no, she didn't have any other questions, and Levy took her back to the reception office, where he asked the secretary to kindly give the young lady a complimentary copy of the works of Charles Smith. Then, without saying another word, he vanished back to his office.

The secretary gave Hope an inscrutable smile and glided into the adjacent room.

Left on her own, Hope simmered with anger. Levy was obviously bluffing. Surely the receptionist had some information about Smith, and as Hope weighed the options of deceit or bribery, her eyes fell on a huge Rolodex sitting on the corner of the desk.

A shiver ran up her spine. She could see the receptionist searching through some shelves with her back to the doorway. Hope had only about ten seconds to act. She flipped up the cover of the Rolodex and located SMITH Charles, with the prophet's full contact information listed: home, office, telephone, fax.

She tore out the card and slunk off without saying goodbye.

53. MISSION

"New York reeks!" was how Hope summed things up as she chewed on a hot dog an inch away from the handset. I immediately asked for a geospatial update.

"I'm in a phone booth at the corner of Fortieth Street and Eighth Avenue."

These particulars evoked no mental picture for me. Between mouthfuls, Hope explained in detail her visit to Levy Publishing, praised the fifty-cent hot dogs served at Bobby's—which I gathered was a nondescript stand on Forty-second Street—and dwelled for a (long) while on the ergonomic virtues of her new Tony Lamas. I tried to visualize the phone bill.

In any case, troop morale seemed high, despite the admittedly slow progress of the investigation. For the time being, all Hope knew was that Charles Smith could be reached at the offices of Mekiddo, a company located in Seattle, Washington.

"What does this company do?"

"No idea."

"Is that all you've got?"

"Yup, that's all."

"Very promising."

"Well, I've gotta run. The bus to Seattle leaves in ten minutes."

"Are you joking?"

"Have I mentioned my new boots? They're really comfortable. You should get some."

This leave-taking filled me with nothing but apprehension. I wanted to dissuade Hope, to convince her to come back, but I just didn't have it in me. It took a lot of courage to stand up to Hope. The most I could manage was to remind her that she had a major calculus exam coming up on Thursday afternoon.

"The mission I'm on," she stated just before hanging up, "is more important than differential calculus."

Hope spent three nights and two days on the road. She crossed three time zones and two watersheds. She changed buses five times, and every bus seemed more run-down and uncomfortable than the one before, but they all had little screens suspended from the ceiling and tuned exclusively to one channel: *Thank You for Travelling with Greyhound.*

She watched the landscape stream past. Cornfield, scrapyard, soybean field, cornfield, incinerator, drive-in theatre, industrial park, Wal-Mart, cornfield, Ford dealer, cornfield, motel, deserted GM factory, empty lot, marshalling yard, soybean field, industrial park, nuclear power plant, cornfield, motel, cement plant, seedy neighbourhoods along the railroad tracks, seedy neighbourhoods under the A-41 interchange, seedy neighbourhoods behind kilometres of chain-link fence, industrial park, river, bungalows, skyscrapers, garbage dumps and countless small animals that had ended their days as roadkill.

When her brain had had enough, Hope did math problems in her head, read the newspapers left behind by other passengers, dozed off curled up in her seat. She subsisted on vending machine fare—the sort of food that is digested in seven minutes and induces fits of hypertension.

Sugar, liquid glucose, cocoa butter, powdered whole milk, hydrogenated vegetable oil, cocoa paste, lactose, powdered skim milk, powdered whey, low-fat cocoa, milk fats, malt extract, salt, emulsifier, soy lecithin, egg white, milk protein, wheat flour and flavouring. Enriched wheat flour, water, sugar and/or glucose-fructose, yeast, vegetable oil (soybean and/or canola), salt, calcium sulphate, esters of diacetyl tartaric acid of mono- and diacylglycerols, mono- and diacylglycerols from vegetable sources, calcium propionate, sodium stearoyl-2-lactylate, corn flour, calcium phosphate, soybean flour, sunflower oil, wheat starch, ammonium phosphate, calcium peroxide, wheat gluten, ethyl alcohol, sorbitol, polysorbate 20, sodium propionate, enzymes, dextrin, cornstarch, carboxymethylcellulose, ammonium sulphate, malt, calcium carbonate, sesame seeds. Vegetable oil (soybean and/or canola), relish (diced cucumbers, glucose-fructose, vinegar, potassium sorbate, xanthan gum, natural flavour (from vegetable sources)), mustard (water, vinegar, mustard seeds, salt, sugar, caramel colouring, spices), water, frozen egg yolks, vinegar, powdered onion, salt, spices, xanthan gum, potassium sorbate, garlic powder, hydrolized vegetable proteins (corn gluten, soybean, wheat gluten), calcium sodium edetate, colouring (paprika).

On the third day at dawn, Hope alighted in Seattle, white as a shard of porcelain. She ingested a burger and took stock of her resources: whitish Tony Lama boots (2), prophet's contact information (1), slightly depleted budget (1).

A game plan started to take shape in her mind.

She bought a map of Greater Seattle and installed herself at the Starbucks to peruse it, downing three bold daily special coffees in a row. There were fifteen or so newspaper vending machines lined up at attention in the hall of the bus terminal, and inside each of them the headline announced the withdrawal of the American troops from the Persian Gulf.

The rush hour was at its peak. People were scurrying in every direction, and Hope realized that, for the first time in her life, she had no schedule or agenda or dosage to follow—only a Mission. It was a happy blend of truancy and crusade. Feeling a sudden lightness, she ordered a fourth coffee and polished her boots with a handful of napkins.

First step: Locate the Mekiddo headquarters. That was easy, since the street was listed in the index of the map. The company was situated on 6th Avenue, in the heart of Chinatown, about a twenty-minute walk. Hope folded the map and set out.

The Mekiddo building offered a classic example of post-industrial architecture. The turquoise facade of synthetic resin—avant-garde during the Vietnam War—had fallen into chronic disrepair. Here and there, shabby brick facing peeped out where a panel was missing. The resin shell must have concealed an old warehouse or a boxing gym or a print shop.

An American flag snapped glumly against its aluminum mast, right next to the battered company name: Mekiddo Corporation Inc. Flanking the name was a rusted logo—a sort of winged lion with the head of a bearded man. An arcane corporate hybrid.

Spray-painted near the door someone had added a piece of unforgiving graffiti: There Were No Good Old Days.

"That's good to know," Hope told herself.

On the surface, Mekiddo might have been an import-export company, a money-laundering operation for drug dealers or a road-engineering firm on the brink of bankruptcy.

Careful not to be conspicuous, Hope hopped from one foot to the other while she sized up the situation. The temperature hovered just above zero, but the dampness went right through her. When the cold finally became unbearable she took shelter in a noodle shop directly across the street.

The restaurant was empty and lunchtime was still a

long way off. She strategically chose a seat by the window and, without taking her eyes off the target, haphazardly ordered a number 17 (lemongrass rice noodles with shrimp). A TV on the counter was tuned to a Vietnamese version of *The Price Is Right*, rebroadcast via satellite, no doubt.

Her number 17 soon arrived. These noodles were nothing like Captain Mofuku's! Hope unsheathed her chopsticks, pushed her three shrimps to the edge of the bowl and began to devour the noodles. Between bites she glanced at the building. Fifteen minutes went by and she had yet to see anyone go through the door.

57. LABYRINTH

Hope crossed the street, dodged the truck of a dried-seahorse dealer and entered the mysterious turquoise building.

Aside from the strange bearded feline's head bolted to the wall, there was no one in the lobby. A fluorescent tube was flashing messages in Morse code. Hope walked up to the reception desk. The chair had evidently been unoccupied for quite a while: abandoned on the imitation granite surface was a Mekiddo-coloured cup lined at the bottom with a cracked layer of coffee, and the newspaper underneath the cup was dated February—the picture on the front page showed the Kuwaiti desert bristling with flaming derricks.

Under the newspaper, Hope found a notebook with the company's organizational chart and a list of the staff's personal extension numbers. She ran her finger down the list until she reached SMITH, Charles—3rd Floor, Section 9, Cubicle 47. The hour of their meeting was at hand.

Hope stepped into the elevator under the menacing gaze of the big cat. The car smelled of oil and linoleum glue, and the machinery creaked in a worrisome way. The doors opened onto a huge space divided into cubicles by movable wall panels. Modular architecture—grey and efficient.

Still not a soul in sight.

In fact, the building looked as if an emergency evacuation had taken place there several weeks earlier. The ceiling was covered with fireproof tiles, some of which had been torn out, exposing bundles of electric wiring.

Hope ventured into the labyrinth and let herself be guided by a sound that was the only sign of life: the squeaking of a poorly lubricated ventilation fan somewhere at the far end of the floor. She wandered around until she came to the realization that this was the third time she had come across the same broken office chair. She was going in circles.

She tried to remember the classic methods for getting out of a labyrinth. Consistently turn left? Draw a map of your movements? Leave a trail of paperclips? More pragmatically, she climbed on a desk to get an overall view of the area.

What she saw in every direction was chaos and desolation. Piles of papers dumped on the desks, abandoned photocopiers, dried-out ivy plants—all covered with a thin film of dust.

Suddenly, Hope cried out: there was a head peeking out over the labyrinth! A few panels away, a man was silently watching her. They eyed each other for several seconds—Hope was about to conclude that she was staring at a mannequin—when the man spoke up.

"Can I help you?"

"Uhh . . . I'm looking for someone."

The man squinted. Hope thought he looked suspicious, but on second thought *she* was the suspicious-looking one, standing there on the desk. She climbed down and headed toward the man by following the directions that he shouted to her over the panels. Right, left, third aisle on the right, then left again.

He was waiting for her in his cubicle, sitting in the shadow of a hill of paperwork topped by a half-full pot of coffee. Hope greeted him with a nod.

"Do you know Charles Smith? I was told he works here."

The man rubbed his chin as he observed Hope. An invisible twenty-four-hour beard rasped under his fingers, and the crooked part in his hair gave him the appearance of a John F. Kennedy gone mad.

"You've got a weird accent. Where are you from?"

"Québec."

"Beg your pardon?"

"Eastern Canada."

A spark of recognition flashed across his face.

"So you speak French! *Je appris le français quand je suis jeune.*"

Hope gave him a polite sign of acknowledgment. Then she pointed to the labyrinth of cubicles with a sweeping gesture: What exactly was this place? The set for a film on Chernobyl? The man found this comparison "funny." This *place*, he explained, was the North American headquarters of the Japanese company Mekiddo—at least, what was left of it, since the offices would be closing for good in exactly (he checked his watch) thirty-seven minutes.

Hope felt a knot in her stomach.

"So Smith doesn't work here any more?"

By way of response, the man tilted his head toward the adjacent cubicle, which had been hastily vacated, like all the others.

Hope dejectedly plunked herself down on a stack of boxes, raising a cloud of dust. She had crossed North America for nothing.

The man chewed on an imaginary toothpick. He did not seem surprised by the situation. On the contrary, one got the distinct impression that he had been expecting this encounter for weeks, that it was his very last assignment and that once Hope exited the building he too could finally leave this place.

He pretended to spit out his toothpick.

"So you're looking for Chuck. And you'd like to talk to him about the end of the world, right?"

58. POOR CHUCK STARTS TO HAVE PROBLEMS

"Coffee?"

He took two Pyrex cups out of the drawer and inspected them under the fluorescent lights. They were almost opaque under the accretion of fingerprints, but this did not seem to bother him, and he proceeded to pour two generous servings of coffee.

"Milk?"

"No thanks."

"You got that right. There is no more milk. They took the fridge away last week."

Hope took a gulp of what assuredly must have been the worst coffee on the entire West Coast. It was bitter, oily and beyond strong, so that from the very first sip she could feel the caffeine percolating into the remote corners of her brain.

Without batting an eyelid the man drained his cup and gave himself a refill. He sniffed and started on his second cup, but this time less hastily. No sound could be heard except for the constant squeaking of the fan and the muffled whine of Boeings flying by directly overhead. Hope looked for a way to kick-start the conversation.

"So you knew Smith?"

"Ah! No one really knew Kamajii."

"Kamajii?"

The man explained that Charles Smith's real name was Hayao Kamajii and that he was from Japan, but that, like so many Asians, he used a Western name to work in the States. In fact, he was an expert mimic: not only was his English flawless—tinged with a slight British accent picked up in Hong Kong—but he had an almost supernatural ability to imitate any accent after only a few minutes.

"In my opinion, he's a bit autistic. All day long I would see him do things like this"—he pretended to twist a paper clip—"for hours at a time. He did origami. He made little drawings."

"What was his job?"

"No idea. I never saw him do any work."

The man took the coffee pot and offered another

round. Hope declined a second too late and found herself holding her sixth coffee of the day.

"One day he tells me he knows the date when the world's going to end. Shows me a manuscript. The man had a strange sense of humour."

"Did you read the manuscript?"

He nodded.

"*Oui*. I remember it mentioned an airport."

"An airport?"

"Yeah. Nice place to wait for the end of the world, huh?"

"I don't fly very often."

He opened a drawer and pulled out an old package of cookies. Then he cautiously took a bite before holding out the package to Hope.

"Cookie?"

She shook her head.

"Anyway, a New York publisher accepts the manuscript and it becomes a bestseller. That's when poor Chuck starts to have problems. The readers don't want just a book—they want a guru. *Alors ils le . . . harassent?*"

"*Harcèlent.*"

"*Oui, ils le harcèlent.* His telephone doesn't stop ringing the whole night. When he leaves his house in the morning, he stumbles over people in sleeping bags: punks, schizophrenics, junkies, COBOL coders."

He bit into another cookie, frowned in disgust and flung the package at the wastebasket, missing the target by several inches. The package smashed against the floor and cookie crumbs flew off in all directions. The man appeared not to notice.

"So this lasts two years. It was crazy! In the end, Chuck just stops going home. He sleeps in the office."

"He slept here?"

"*Oui*. Sitting in his office chair."

Hope scanned the surrounding area. The coffee was distorting her vision. The slightest object was fringed with a pink and blue halo, like a 3-D movie. She felt little electric sparks crackling around her nostrils and reverberating down to the bottom of her lungs. That last coffee had definitely been one too many.

"Has he been gone for very long?"

"Nine months. Eight, maybe. I can give you his new business card, if you want."

He swung his chair around, fished about in the mass of papers pinned to the cubicle wall and extracted a rectangular piece of pasteboard.

Hope carefully examined Kamajii's card—English on one side, Japanese on the other. She took a deep breath to ward off her nausea. All around, the cubicles and the furniture seemed to vibrate. Hope was in a video game, standing in front of the Gates of Heaven, and she was about to be teleported ten thousand floors away.

59. SUPERCHARGED

Business card in hand, Hope charged through the glass doors on the ground floor and spewed an ambiguous blend of bile and coffee against the turquoise tiles right at the foot of the bearded lion.

She spat several times, wiped her mouth with an old handkerchief, and leaned against the wall, gasping for breath and sweating despite the freezing rain. She wanted to be back home.

Hope pocketed the business card and then, supercharged on coffee, shot away like a bullet and marched for several minutes in a straight line. She eventually bumped against the A-frame signboard of a travel agency announcing unbeatable prices for last-minute tickets. Hope walked in with no second thoughts. The next scene unfolded as if in a dream, half in Mandarin, half in English. As it happened, the agency actually was selling a ticket at half price—an eleventh-hour cancellation, a deal not to be missed, departure at 3:23 p.m. Hope pulled the envelope out of her bag and slapped a wad of bills down on the counter.

Five minutes later she hopped into a cab and zoomed off to the airport.

60. YOU ARE LEAVING THE AMERICAN SECTOR

I had just eaten when the telephone rang in the Bunker. I dove over the couch, grabbed the handset and accepted the charges. Hope was in the international departures area of the Seattle airport. Her flight was leaving in fifteen minutes.

"Which flight?"

"US Airways 1212 to Tokyo."

I rubbed my eyes, trying to digest this new information. Hope's voice moved closer to the telephone then away from it and was in danger of disappearing at any moment. The soundtrack behind her included a fuzzy voice enumerating flight and gate numbers. I pictured flight information boards clicking out all the destinations in the world.

Hope talked about her Mission, her meeting with John F. Kennedy and the enigmatic Mekiddo corporation. But I wasn't really paying attention, being too busy sizing up the magnitude of the situation. Alone at the opposite end of the continent, noticeably under the influence of caffeine, Hope was preparing to take off for Tokyo.

"What are you going to do there, *exactly*?"

She hesitated for a second.

"Don't know yet. I'll see once I get there."

"You'll see once you're there?!"

"Don't worry. I've gotta run now. They just made the final boarding call."

Standing by myself in the dim light of the Bunker, I pondered that uncharacteristic hesitation and the vagueness of her answer. I couldn't imagine Hope letting herself get swept along by events. It just wasn't like her—there was much more Hope than Randall in her.

She must have had a plan up her sleeve. A secret plan embedded in her mind at an impossible angle, designed to travel express with no stops along the way.

A plan with enough room for just one person.

61. MAY I BORROW YOUR GAS MASK?

Hope opened her eyes just in time to see the final seconds of a short travel film entitled *Between Tradition and Modernism*. Her ears were buzzing. In her lap was the emergency procedures brochure showing passengers fleeing from fire, asphyxiation, drowning—please remain calm.

The pilot announced the final descent in picturesque English. It was 3:32 p.m. local time, practically the same time Hope had left Seattle. But this was 3:32 *tomorrow*. By virtue of an amusing temporal sleight of hand somewhere in the middle of the Pacific, passengers and crew had leap-frogged over twenty-four hours.

Hope released the pressure in her eardrums and reset her watch, fascinated by the idea that an entire day had literally vanished into thin air.

The 747 made a faultless approach over Narita airport and softly touched down. As the plane slowly taxied toward the gate, Hope scanned the tarmac through the porthole: dozens of square kilometres of concrete, tanks of kerosene, beat-up baggage carts. Here and there, members of the ground crew walked around, dressed in high-tech overalls, ears covered with huge shells, eyes protected by dark glasses. They looked like people working in a toxic environment.

Around the terminal, Hope counted about forty 747s, each of them bearing the colours of a different airline: Saudi Arabian Airlines, Aeroflot, Lufthansa, Aerolíneas Argentinas, Qantas, TAM, Air China, American Airlines, Delta, Air India.

After she got off the plane, Hope went along the corridor that led to the immigration counters. There was an endless, tightly packed line of travellers, coiled like the small intestine of some fantastic beast. Hope heard people speaking English, Japanese, Portuguese, Russian, Chinese. Two men with New Zealand accents were discussing the range of a 747. A young woman was reading yesterday's

República. Some kids were squabbling in Mandarin. Babel, upside down.

In his glass cage, an immigration officer inspected Hope's passport without making the slightest comment and stamped it with a ninety-day tourist visa. Wham! Welcome to the land of ramen.

She walked straight past the baggage carousels and into the arrivals area.

First stop, the foreign exchange office, where she bought ¥29,092 (before the three per cent commission). The figure seemed astronomical, but Hope kept in mind that this stack of bills was worth just US$200. She examined a ¥5,000 note, holding it up against the light. It was anybody's guess how much range such a sum could provide in a city like Tokyo. A week? Two days? Ten minutes?

She slipped the money into her back pocket, twisted the transaction receipt and lobbed it at the nearest trashcan but missed. When she bent down to collect the piece of paper, she almost knocked her head against a nailclipper vending machine.

Japan promised to be strange.

Hope mentally converted the prices displayed on the vending machine. She was stunned by the results. Who could afford to clip their nails in this country?

She turned away from the machine and surveyed the arrivals area. Every so often, the public address system transmitted messages in Japanese. It was the first time Hope found herself in a place where she could not understand a single word. She needed to get her hands on a phrase book, one of those vacuous lexicons listing all the commonplaces of commercial tourism. Where can I find a hotel? How much is this kimono / vase / knife? I am looking for the train station / post office / washroom. Thank you, that is very kind of you. Goodbye.

Hope stepped into a newsstand and, with a great deal of gesturing and a few snippets of English, managed to get her point across to the cashier, who suggested *Rough Planet Tokyo*. The guidebook included a section of ready-made phrases, for example: "Where is the nearest bunker?" (*Sumimasen, kono atari ni chika sherutaa wa ari masu ka?*) or "May I borrow your gas mask / anti-radiation suit?" (*Gasumasuku / houshanou bougyo suutsu o kari te mo ii desu ka?*)

Japan promised to be very strange indeed.

62. THE GREAT PRIMAL SOUP

Sitting in the subway car, Hope scrutinized Hayao Kamajii's business card for the umpteenth time. She opened her *Rough Planet* guide and studied the map of downtown Tokyo, in the middle of which she had marked the (theoretical) location of the Mekiddo offices with a red X. It had taken her nearly a half-hour to decipher the address printed on the business card. Not that she lacked a sense of direction—the guidebook devoted an entire chapter to the Japanese address system, which was apt to drive even an astrophysicist crazy.

The subway gradually filled up as it approached the city centre. Hope noticed that a number of the passengers wore surgical masks. What did they know that she didn't? She flipped through her guidebook: "Do you know where some antibiotics / morphine can be found?" (*Moruhine / kousei busshitsu ha doko de te ni hairu ka shitte masu ka?*)

She began to chew on her fingernails and found they had a funny taste.

The last few days had zipped by so quickly that Hope had denied the existence of her own body. She took a moment to inspect her hands, something she had not done since leaving New York. The electric blue varnish was peeling and the nail of her right index finger was cracked, not to mention all the grunge that had built up day after day. Underneath, millions of bacteria, spores and germs were napping, and with a good microscope it would have been possible to reconstitute her itinerary from Norbert Vong's smoky kitchen to the Narita Airport, with all the stops and stages in between: Sammy Levy's office, the Greyhound bus ride, various vending machines spread throughout the northern United States, the noodle shop in Seattle's Chinatown and the unending flight on the US Airways 747.

For a second, Hope imagined that the chewed-off bits of her nails had been sent to a virgin, lifeless planet, like the Earth at the time of the great primal soup. Perhaps they would contaminate that nourishing environment and engender new life forms there. First to appear would be the one-celled organisms, then jellyfish, then teeming vertebrate fish, swimming and crawling, emerging from the oceans, developing technologies and languages and religions and cities and, ultimately, civilizations that would war against each other and build spiral towers and live in fear of the end of the world. A whole world born out of a few grungy bits of fingernail.

Hope was suddenly sorry she hadn't invested in a nail clipper.

63. CUL-DE-SAC

Hope changed lines three times and resurfaced on Akko Boulevard. The streets were packed, yet the area did not look like a commercial district: no skyscrapers, no hordes of salarymen or messengers, but lots of restaurants, boutiques, laundries, bookstores. Certainly not the kind of neighbourhood Hope would have associated with the headquarters of a multinational corporation.

The display window of an electronics store attracted her attention. Behind the glass, a dozen screens rebroadcasted a dozen channels: ten times ten derricks aflame in the Kuwaiti desert.

She took her bearings and set out in the direction indicated by the address numbers. After ten minutes of deduction and triangulation, she halted at the spot where, indisputably, the Mekiddo offices should have stood. But instead of the lion with the bearded human head there was some sort of swimming pool or Turkish bath. She backtracked and checked the street signs three times. The address still seemed to jibe with her calculations. Had she made a mistake?

She pushed open the glass door. The lobby was suffused with the odour of chlorine and disinfectant. A young man seated at the cash was completely engrossed in a novel. He spoke a little English, and Hope asked him if she could go in to see the pool. He made an ambiguous gesture that she took for a yes.

Alone in the women's locker room, Hope carefully examined the faucets, the counters, the tiles. Everything was brand new and sparkling.

Hope removed her boots and followed the corridor leading to the pool. What she found there was far from exotic, but given the total absence of bathers, the atmosphere was vaguely unsettling. Perched on his tall chair, the lifeguard was snoozing. Behind him, the alignment of the buoys on the wall was so perfect as to appear surreal.

Whatever this place was, it was obviously not the Mekiddo mother ship.

When she returned to the lobby, Hope showed the business card to the cashier. Had she erred in her calculations? The young man shook his head: This was the right spot, but the Mekiddo offices had moved three months ago.

Where?

The young man, who seemed to find the question very amusing, plunged into his book again without answering.

Back on the sidewalk, Hope was somewhat shaken. This investigation was shaping up to be more complicated than what she had expected. She looked at her watch, opened her *Rough Planet* to the chapter on accommodations, and found a youth hostel a two-minute walk away, at the end of a cul-de-sac.

It was a narrow, quiet street, evidently inhabited by working people, since Hope did not cross paths with anyone except a Jordanian—or possibly Syrian—cleaning lady. In other words, she said to herself, it was a good place to set up a headquarters. But instead of a youth hostel, what she found was a vacant lot closed off from the street by a fence.

She verified the surrounding addresses several times. She had not made any navigational errors—the hostel had disappeared. Did anything ever stay put in this city?

Hope let out an extended yawn. A blend of sleepiness and nausea began to overtake her. She spotted a bar on the ground floor of a crumbling building stuck between a Buddhist temple and a fruit store. A neon light sputtered around a very un-Japanese-looking name: Jaffa's.

The building appeared to be on the brink of collapse, but the storefront looked inviting. Hope stepped inside.

The interior was bathed in a comforting half-light. "Sir Duke" was playing softly and two students were sipping beers in a booth, surrounded by books. A girl stood behind the counter. Mid-thirties, Mao-collar shirt, dreadlocks tied up in a bun, cigarette suspended from the corner of her mouth. She was drying the glasses with an air of nonchalant virility probably picked up from a John Wayne movie.

Hope noticed a pay phone on the wall near the toilets. She tottered up to it and grabbed on to it as if it were a lifebuoy. She opened her *Rough Planet*, dropped a few coins in the slot and dialed the youth hostel number. A peculiar dial tone gave way to a recorded message in Japanese—a long, unfathomable message. She hung up, and the telephone regurgitated the yen.

Hope rubbed her eyes, glanced unenthusiastically at the list of youth hostels in the neighbourhood. Her mind began to blur. She brought her left hand up to her lips and absentmindedly chewed on the nail of her forefinger. She frowned and spat: her fingernail tasted of polish. She eyed the girl at the bar. Maybe she had some nail clippers.

She dropped all her change into the pay phone and punched in the Bunker's number. A few seconds went by. An operator eventually took the call and launched into a non-stop explanation in high-speed Japanese. Something was obviously amiss. The number may have been incomplete, or she had not put in enough yen or, then again, maybe the tectonic plate of North America had sunk into the magma.

She looked at the *Rough Planet* table of contents, found the "How to dial a telephone number" section, sighing. She would have to learn everything over again from scratch.

A huge weight bore down on her shoulders. She was done in, no longer willing to struggle against matter, let alone a Japanese telephone operator. She hung up. Yawned. Leaned against the wall. She gently let herself slide down and dropped onto her heels with her eyes shut. "Just a quick nap," she muttered. "A quick tiny little nap."

64. 1945

Hope opened her eyes in a panic. She was lying on a futon under a heavy quilt. Where was she?

She propped herself up on one elbow and looked around: tatami, sliding rice paper doors, cabinets camouflaged in the walls—a veritable museum of traditional Japanese architecture. There was a bathroom at one end and a kitchenette at the other, with a fireplace unobtrusively heating the apartment.

Who would have thought that houses like this still existed in Japan? It looked like a movie set, but one where the realistic effect had been pushed to the limit by an obsessive designer. The wood showed subtle signs of wear in the places touched time and again by a passing hand. The edges of the tatami were threadbare. A complex smell of wax, starch and soap pervaded the room.

So it definitely wasn't a movie set. Someone lived here.

Next to the futon, an overturned wooden crate served as a night table. On it lay a flashlight, an ashtray holding three dubious cigarette butts (Dubek No. 9) and a bilingual (Arabic–English) edition of *A Thousand and One Nights*. On the floor, a few dozen books stacked against a wall included French, English, Japanese and Hebrew titles. Hope opened an edition of the Talmud and ran a perplexed finger over the austere blocks of Hebrew lettering. Just who was the person who lived here?

She found her clothes and bag neatly folded at the foot of the bed. While she dressed, she examined the room with growing disbelief. No electrical appliances of any sort—not even a switch or light bulb. Just the fireplace quietly burning. On the wall hung a yellowed calendar opened to August 1945.

Hope felt dizzy: What if she had actually been thrust back in time? She nervously shuffled through the bills and magazines scattered on a small desk, and sighed with relief when she finally came upon an edition of *Ha'aretz* dated March 12, 1991.

She explored the house on tiptoe. It was hardly any bigger than the Randall Pet Shop. But it was oh, so much more tasteful! She marvelled at the washroom, especially the sunken blue ceramic bath. Perched on the tiny toilet was a box of sanitary napkins. Hope registered the clue: the occupant was a woman.

When she looked in the mirror, Hope discovered a wreck with dark rings around the eyes and cracked lips. She splashed water on her face and washed her hands. Her fingernails brought a scowl of disgust to her face. She opened the taps of the bathtub and, from a basket serving as medicine cabinet, pulled out a nail clipper and a bottle of nail polish remover. While the hot water was running, she cleaned, cut and filed her fingernails with painstaking precision. The clippings showered down on the floor tiles amid the gentle fragrance of keratin and steam.

After a while, Hope was enveloped in a sweet empti-ness. She tested the temperature of the water, took off her clothes and slid into the tub. A faint smile lit up her face. She took a deep breath and let herself sink below the surface.

65. AN IMPOSSIBLE ANGLE

The Tony Lamas were waiting dutifully by the door. The leather felt cold under the soles of her feet, but now properly shod, Hope regained a sense of control over events.

Once outside, she leaped into the future. The little traditional house—all rustic pine, rice paper and slate tiles—sat on the roof of a building, several floors above Tokyo!

The sun was at its highest and the light made Hope squint. Her environment grew more distinct. A deck of greyish wood, synthetic resin furniture, a few empty flowerpots and a miniature Shinto altar (long unused, if the stubs of incense planted in the sand were any indication). The surrounding roof offered a depressing landscape: tarred gravel, discoloured tiles, braids of electric wire and dozens of parabolic dishes and Yagi antennas.

A few kilometres away stood a thicket of waterfront cranes, which immediately brought back images of Yarmouth. Hope sniffed the air for traces of iodine, but the only smell the wind brought her was of diesel.

Hope moved closer to the ledge and looked straight down. A fire escape zigzagged its way to an alley, five storeys below, where she could make out a hopscotch court drawn in pink chalk, and a pair of dumpsters.

How the hell had she landed on top of this building? Someone must have carried her up here, but how?

On inspecting the house more closely, she discovered a concrete staircase flanked by an old water heater. She opened the door a crack and cast a glance down something resembling a mineshaft. She swept her hand over the wall and flipped the switch. An ancient fluorescent tube started to blink two floors below.

The stairway was barely wide enough for one person. It plunged directly into the building—no landing, no door, no handrail—at an impossible angle, as if the inner wall had been bored through to make the roof accessible from ground level without the need to stop on the floors in between.

A secret stairway.

66. AN INCREASING TOLERANCE FOR THE UNLIKELY

Hope emerged in the back room of Jaffa's. The bar was still closed and there was a tape of reggae music playing for no one in particular. "Come We Go Burn Down Babylon."

The girl she had glimpsed the day before was busy behind the counter. She was wearing a tattered Pac-Man T-shirt and had her hair up in a loose knot. She greeted

Hope with a warm smile. Bob Marley continued to chant down Babylon.

The girl wiped her hands on her T-shirt and lowered the volume.

"Bon matin, camarade!"

So, she spoke French . . . Hope wondered whether this should come as a surprise. No, ultimately, she was not really surprised. She realized that over the last few days she had shown an increasing tolerance for the unlikely and the improbable.

"Feeling better? You had nightmares all night long."

"What time is it?"

"Almost noon. Are you hungry?"

Before Hope could say anything, the girl peeled opened a container of ramen, unscrewed the top of a thermos bottle and poured some boiling water on the noodles, which released a pungent aroma of buckwheat, seaweed and monosodium glutamate. She placed the bowl on the counter with a theatrical flourish.

Hope immediately recognized the irksome little astronaut on the label, but never had the smell of a mundane package of ramen made her mouth water to such an extent! She sat down on the stool, grabbed the chopsticks with sudden virtuosity and began bolting the noodles down at an unreasonable rate. The girl burst out laughing.

"Easy now! You look like you haven't eaten anything for weeks! Is that why you fainted yesterday afternoon?"

"I didn't faint. I fell asleep."

"Well, you sleep very soundly, comrade! I had to lug you up five flights of stairs on my back!"

Hope eyed the girl between mouthfuls of noodles. She did not look very Japanese, but it may simply have been the rasta hairdo that muddied the picture.

"So the samurai hut on the roof—you live there?"

"Cool, isn't it? It's the house where my boss grew up. He had it moved from Kokura in the fifties. A team of archaeologists dismantled it piece by piece. You can still see the numbers on some of the planks."

"That's bizarre."

"Yeah, I agree. But it suits me fine. The boss never sets foot in Tokyo, so the house serves as lodging for the bar personnel. The personnel being yours truly."

She reached her hand out over the counter.

"By the way, I'm Merriam."

"Hope."

Smiles, handshake. Merriam took a bag of lemons out of the fridge and emptied it on the counter. Then she began slicing the citrus into quarters using an over-sized knife.

"So, what brings you to Tokyo? Sightseeing? Business? Love?"

"I'm looking for someone. A man called Hayao Kamajii. Is that a common name?"

Merriam bit into a section of lemon and puckered her face.

"Kind of. There must be about nine thousand of them in the phone book."

67. RAID

Merriam listened attentively to Hope's account of her misadventures. She examined Kamajii's business card and confirmed the address. She was very familiar with the municipal swimming pool that Hope was referring to, but she had no recollection of seeing the Mekiddo offices there.

"That said, I know where they are."

"Really?"

"Yes. In Nayot, the district just next to this one."

She glanced at the clock on the microwave oven.

"I've still got an hour to spare. If you like, we can go check it out right now."

Without waiting for an answer, she reached into a narrow cupboard and pulled out a water-lily green folding bicycle. Hope gulped down the broth of her noodles in one go and mechanically noted the best-before date printed on the rim of the bowl of ramen: 17 07 01. The Mission was still on track.

Merriam lifted the roll-up grille halfway and they slipped into the street. The spring sunshine beat down on the surrounding facades. Hope discovered a Tokyo completely different from the one she had seen the day before.

Merriam lowered the grille again, swiftly unfolded the bicycle, and a minute later they were flying through the streets of the neighbourhood, with Merriam steering and Hope precariously balanced on the rack. It was a mild day, and the thoroughfare was overrun by schoolgirls in shirtsleeves with their sweaters knotted around their waists.

Leaning over Merriam's shoulder, Hope observed the streets.

"About Mekiddo—exactly what sort of company is it?"

Merriam shook her head.

"No idea, comrade."

Merriam obviously knew the district inside out. They rode up Akko Boulevard, weaved in and out among the cars, sped across vast, overcrowded intersections like a bullet, threaded their way along a cluttered lane, cut across an inner courtyard, barrelled down three stairs (for an instant Hope lost contact with the bike), jumped over a median strip and rolled under a monorail ramp. Merriam flashed Hope a reassuring smile over her shoulder.

"We're almost there!"

They careened around the corner and braked in front of a commercial building. With her heart pounding, Hope instantly caught sight of the strange bearded Mekiddo mascot. Next to the beast, however, hung a large sign advertising the upcoming construction of thirty-seven luxury condominiums, which the idyllic illustration made instantly understandable, even for someone without the slightest notion of Japanese. The doors were boarded up. Fifty metres away, three pink excavators with white polka dots were tearing bites of concrete and steel reinforcement rods out of the side of the building.

Merriam spat on the sidewalk.

"*Beitzim!*"

She pulled a cellphone out of her pocket and dialed the directory assistance number. After a heated discussion with an unspecified interlocutor—secretary or telephone operator—Merriam hung up and checked her watch with a worried expression.

"They've moved to the Gotah borough."

"Is it far?"

"Yes, quite. We'll have to put the investigation off to another day."

The excavators were working at a good clip, rather gracefully, too. It brought to mind some sort of dance, a demolition ballet. Merriam took a pack of Dubek No. 9 out of her pocket and offered one to Hope, who shook her head. A match, a puff. They looked on as a section of wall crashed down in a cloud of dust. The smell of rubble spread around them, and Hope automatically brought the nail of her ring finger to her lips. But that morning's manicure had left her incisors with nothing to sink into.

68. MUTATION

The mystery deepened. This was already the second time that Mekiddo had disappeared, and Merriam swore she had seen this place humming with activity only a few days earlier.

No matter how tolerant she had become toward the unlikely and the improbable, Hope refused to accept that a multinational corporation could, in no more than seventy-two hours, move several hundred employees, chairs and desks, flotillas of photocopiers, kilos of paper clips, potted ferns, water dispensers, coffee machines, sandwich vending machines—in total, a quantity of matter and biomass equivalent to the weight of a small iceberg.

Merriam did not seem especially surprised. She dragged on her cigarette as she watched the excavators working.

"They are razing Tokyo, comrade. One piece at a time."

The way she saw it, Tokyo was in constant mutation. Nothing stayed still for very long and the landscape was metamorphosing at a mind-boggling pace. You could go down the same street every morning, and then, from one day to the next, not recognize it any more.

"But there aren't as many construction sites since the Nikkei crashed. And, in fact, they're predicting the most severe real estate devaluation in decades, to be accompanied by a wave of suicides."

"That bad?"

"That bad. And that's just for starters. I could show you real estate not too far from here where the square metre was going for a million dollars last summer. Japan is going downhill fast."

She hesitated, seemingly on the verge of adding something, but changed her mind. She smoked half her cigarette and then flicked the smoking butt into the back of a passing truck.

69. MODERN ART

"Are you sure you'll be able to find your way back?" Merriam asked three times as they stood on the corner of Akko Boulevard, about to part company for the afternoon.

Hope assured her that, yes, there was no problem—she had her *Rough Planet* in her pocket. Merriam nevertheless insisted on marking the phone number of the Jaffa on Hope's forearm, just in case.

"Which area are you planning to go to?"

Hope sniffed the air.

"Oh, I've got something in mind."

She started on her way and pondered Tokyo's instability in general and the disappearance of the Mekiddo offices in particular. She soon let herself get drawn into the environment: the display windows, the ever-present mascots, the restaurant menus, the screens, the faces of the passersby. She stopped in front of the door of a pachinko parlour. Techno music, neon lights, the roar of the steel balls. What *was* this place? For a moment, she considered going in and, guidebook at the ready, addressing the players.

"Where can I acquire a machete / machine-gun / rocket launcher?" (*Na ta / mashin gan / roketto hou ha doko de te ni hairi masu ka?*)

On second thought, maybe it wasn't such a good idea.

One or two kilometres farther, Hope passed under a highway, absently kicking a few dead pigeons, and arrived at the port. A vast intermodal complex stretched away on both sides of the harbour: thousands of multicoloured containers stacked up on top of each other. Maersk, Hapag-Lloyd, Hanjin and China Shipping. Everywhere the landscape was the same.

Walking along the chain-link fence, she watched the activity on the other side. Forklifts scurrying around, droning like huge beetles. Workers shouting over the noise. The clanging of metal. Various rumbling noises. And in the background, the hulking orange mass of the *Aron Habrit*, a container ship in the process of being unloaded.

Hope passed the wall of containers and continued on to the unloading area. A crew of longshoremen were extricating a bulky object from a battered container in order to load it onto a truck. Posted at a sensible distance, three men in business suits watched the scene while exchanging remarks.

Curious to see the object that would soon come into view, Hope leaned against the fence. An old Korean tank? Gold ingots? A freeze-dried mammoth? In any case, the thing was awfully heavy, judging by the groans of the hoist.

What emerged from the container, centimetre by centimetre, was a concrete monolith. The surface was scarred and the edges bristled with the rusted stumps of steel rods. One side was completely covered with an interlacing of colourful graffiti, which to Hope looked vaguely familiar.

Before Hope's eyes was an enormous fragment of the *Grenzmauer* newly arrived from Berlin!

With her fingers hooked into the chain-links, she watched in disbelief. What was this artefact doing in Tokyo?

She tried to ask the workers, but none of them spoke English and her guidebook was not at all helpful

"Can you help me? I'm injured / infected / contagious." (*Kega o shi te i masu / osen sa re te i masu / kansen shi te i masu. Te o kashi te morae masu ka?*)

One of the business-suited men crossed the loading zone and came toward Hope with a friendly expression. They exchanged small bows of the head. He explained that the section of wall, a gift of the Bundesrepublik Deutschland to the Tokyo prefecture, would soon be part of the permanent exhibition of the city's Museum of Modern Art.

The Berlin Wall—modern art? Hope tried to mask her bewilderment.

The hoist operator deposited the precious object on the truck bed as softly as a snowflake. The truck's suspension sagged with a painful creak. Immediately, the longshoremen strapped the fragment down on the bed, while the men in suits signed various papers.

The truck lurched away and lumbered onto the boulevard with its two tons of Cold War. A moment later it disappeared in a curve, behind a bulwark of containers.

Brushing the palm of her hand over her shirt pocket, Hope felt the reassuring bulge of the nail clipper.

It was nearly midnight when Hope came within sight of the Jaffa. The only source of light in the narrow lane was the window of a laundry, as blue and spectral as a chunk of iceberg. The bar's neon signs were turned off and the steel grille was rolled halfway down. Stationed near the entrance, Merriam was smoking a cigarette.

"Do you realize what time it is? I was worried."

Hope rubbed her arms under the thin cloth of her blouse.

"It's freezing!"

"Of course it's freezing! It *is* still March! Come on, I've just made some tea."

Hope slipped under the grille, which Merriam closed behind her with a hefty shove. Two twists of the key and they were sheltered from looters and the living dead. As far as bunkers went, this one was unbeatable. Reggae music in the background, chairs tipped up on the tables, the unobtrusive swish of the dishwasher. Near the cash register a large teapot released a graceful question mark of steam.

Merriam tossed an old University of Tel Aviv sweat-shirt on the counter, and Hope, shivering, pulled it over her head.

"Still, you might have given me a call."

"I got slightly lost."

"Didn't you have your guidebook?"

"The layout of the streets doesn't make any sense!"

"Yeah, it takes some getting used to."

"I was on the wrong block. For a while I thought the Jaffa had been razed to the ground during the afternoon and replaced by a Holiday Inn."

Merriam smiled and poured two glasses of tea.

"There's no chance of that happening. The City of Tokyo put this crumbling shack on its list of protected heritage sites in 1971."

"I find that hard to believe."

"It's one of the few buildings from the Edo period that has survived the 1923 earthquake, the 1945 bombing raids and the urban renewal wave of the 1960s. You can't change so much as a lock without a permit. Speaking of which . . ."

She took a heavy set of keys out of a drawer and slipped off an old copper key, which she handed to Hope.

"From now on, if you ever find the steel grille locked, you can just go up the emergency stairway."

Hope thanked her with a nod. The reggae music ebbed and flowed on the speakers, disappearing from time to time—a tidal movement typical of overused cassette tapes. While Hope warmed her hands on the cup of tea, Merriam began to add up the contents of the cash register.

"Need any help?"

"Thanks, but it's not a problem. The sales never add up to very much."

The Jaffa, Merriam explained as she mechanically smoothed out ¥1000 bills between her thumb and index finger, was located smack in the middle of the Sargasso Sea: a gyre bounded by three metro stations, eight hotels and one of the Tokyo University campuses. The surrounding neighbourhood swarmed with students, convention delegates and North American tourists, yet the Jaffa was unable to tap into this clientele. Whenever customers happened to wander in, it was because they were looking for something else. A phantom youth hostel, for instance.

The bar's clientele was made up exclusively of regulars, mostly anthropology students who nursed their beers for hours while reviewing their course notes. As a result, the proceeds were chronically thin and the profit was nil. In fact, the place operated at a loss every other month, a situation to which the owner seemed completely indifferent. This, according to Merriam, lent credence to the tax-shelter hypothesis.

"He bought the bar in the late fifties. At the time, he owned a small light bulb factory in Kobe. Today he manufactures printed circuits in three countries. So he may have totally forgotten that he owns this building. In any case, I've never seen him."

"Never?"

"Never. The accountant comes to check the books every quarter and takes a look at the inventory. It almost never takes more than twenty minutes. In other words, we're in the blind spot. Which reminds me—would you like to call Canada?"

"Call Canada?"

"Your family. Your friends. Your boyfriend. Anyone you like. In any case, just feel free to use the bar phone. The bill disappears on one of the boss's six hundred accounts."

She arranged the bundles of money as she spoke and then scribbled some numbers on a piece of paper, slipped the (meagre) earnings into an envelope and locked everything into a small safe hidden under the counter. Then she rubbed her hands together in satisfaction and glanced at the clock. Twenty past midnight. Out of a drawer she pulled a large cloth-bound edition of the Torah, which concealed a bag of tender green buds, a pack of rolling papers and a plastic lighter.

Hope watched her crush a bud and blend it with tobacco on the cover of the Torah, brush a small amount into a piece of the thin paper and roll it with her thumbs. She flicked her tongue back and forth across the edge of the paper, and voilà! Then, like some manic engineer, she examined the joint to ensure it was properly shaped. Hope smiled and took a gulp of tea.

"Nice work!"

"Thanks. I've had lots of spare time since I moved to Japan."

The smell of sulphur and resin floated into the air. Merriam took two ceremonious puffs and offered the joint to Hope, who declined with a little wave.

"You're wrong not to accept. It's an excellent remedy for jet lag. What's more, this stuff is aeroponic: the plants grow with their roots exposed to the air. A method developed by the Japanese Space Agency to make farming possible in a weightless environment."

Hope laughed.

"Who'd want to farm in a weightless environment?"

"Good question. I guess it would be someone who had doubts about the future of the planet."

71. CARPET BOMBING

An oceanic wind swept over the roof of the building and the sound of ten highways kilometres away was clearly audible, rumblings transported by the biting cold.

Leaning against the guardrail, Hope admired the city lights—billions of lumens, radiating and then evaporating in space. Tokyo was no doubt visible from the moon.

Merriam yawned and pulled out a pack of No. 9. A flash of the lighter and then there was another little red light shining in Tokyo.

"The Americans tested napalm around here, you know."

"Oh?"

"A few months before Hiroshima. Everything you see around us, forty square kilometres—levelled. In one night. A B-29 every two minutes. Eight tons of bombs per plane. I'll let you do the arithmetic."

The tip of the cigarette pulsated against the darkness like a heartbeat, appearing almost alive.

"According to the census there were forty thousand people per square kilometre living in this district. Large families crowded into houses made of wood and paper."

"Like this house?"

"Not really, no, but the materials used were similar. Once the fire started it was impossible to put out. Also, napalm has the consistency of jelly. It sticks to clothing, and hair."

She took two long drags on her cigarette.

"When the bombardment ended, at about five in the morning, the U.S. Air Force had killed a hundred thousand people and left a million homeless. In military jargon it's called carpet bombing. You flatten the landscape down to carpet level."

Hope fought back a shiver, either from horror or the cold—she couldn't quite tell.

"Hard to believe it happened right here . . ."

Merriam took one last puff and rubbed her cigarette

out in a muddy ashtray standing near the Shinto shrine.

"Wait a minute, I think I have a picture."

They took off their shoes and went inside the house. Merriam brought out a battery lamp and a gas radiator. The radiator coughed a little as it started up. Merriam rubbed her hands for a moment in the lukewarm breath of the heater. Then she searched through her bookcase and drew out a large illustrated book.

The History of Tokyo, she translated.

She riffled the pages and stopped on an aerial photo of the neighbourhood taken the day after the bombing. A cemetery, or a crater—no, more like a mass grave. It was possible to make out the bodies heaped together in the streets and at the intersections. And in the exact centre of the still-smoking scene was the building that now housed the Jaffa, inexplicably upright.

Merriam unrolled the futon with a kick and flopped down on her back without bothering to look for a pillow or a quilt.

"The building survived due to a combination of factors. On the north side, the adjacent building had already burned, and there was a lane on the south side that served as a firebreak. Miraculous, all the same."

She yawned, groped around until she found her pack of No. 9, stuck a last cigarette between her lips and forgot to light it. A second later she was asleep.

Standing in the middle of the room, Hope was unable to tear herself away from the sight of those hundreds of bodies, blackened and twisted beyond recognition, piled on top of each other like dead branches. A dress rehearsal for the end of days.

72. IN SPACE AND TIME

Hope liked Merriam, and vice versa, even though they basically knew almost nothing about each other. Merriam asked no questions—at any rate, no tactless questions (why Hope never called Canada, for example)—and when asked about her own life, she usually broke her answers off in mid-sentence.

All the information that Hope had patiently gleaned could fit into a short paragraph.

Born in Jerusalem in the midfifties, Merriam grew up in a kibbutz on the Negev plateau. Her mother was an agronomist and her father, Japanese. She lived in Tel Aviv, and then Greece, studied archaeology at the Sorbonne for several years before finally settling in Tokyo in 1987 at the beginning of the economic bubble. The yen was strong then, the Nikkei went soaring into a cloudless sky, and there was a labour shortage throughout the archipelago.

But economic bubble or not, Hope was no closer to

unravelling the mystery as to what may have prompted someone with a Ph.D. in archaeology from the Sorbonne to come eke out a living in a seedy Tokyo bar. Perhaps the explanation lay in those unopened fancy envelopes from the Israeli embassy that were gathering dust on the table.

Merriam was a woman of contradictions. For instance, she could hold forth on carbon dating, the human genome or infrared photography, and then, the very next minute, smoke a joint as long as your arm and listen to Stevie Wonder with the volume cranked up, while staring into space (what she called "taking leave of the planet"). She never left the Jaffa except to do her shopping in the neighbourhood, yet she still knew Tokyo like the back of her hand. And not once had she asked Hope why she insisted on meeting Hayao Kamajii, which did not prevent Merriam from going all-out to support Hope's Mission.

The weeks passed with each day looking much like the day before.

Every morning, Hope and Merriam woke up at dawn (which, in Merriam's time zone, meant ten o'clock), grabbed a quick breakfast, called directory assistance, asked for the new address of the Mekiddo Kabushiki Gaisha, please, chose a means of transport (bicycle, metro, Tony Lamas) and dashed over to the aforementioned address.

Unfortunately, the directory assistance databases always lagged a few hours—sometimes days—behind reality. With each sortie, Hope and Merriam found themselves looking at buildings that were abandoned or for sale, vacant spaces, makeshift parking lots, demolition sites or, more rarely, brand-new buildings that had sprung up overnight like mushrooms.

This business went on repeatedly for two weeks, at which point Merriam decided that it would be smarter to call Mekiddo directly, speak to Kamajii and arrange to meet him.

But being smart did not make much difference in this pursuit.

Because, while it was easy to speak to a receptionist at Mekiddo, as soon as you scratched below the surface, the situation became tricky. Every phone call went astray in the convoluted telephone system, ended up at the wrong extension or in a voice mailbox that did not accept any messages, please call back later. Often, the connection would be cut off without warning. Conversely, at other times it was Merriam who gave up, exasperated after listening for forty-five minutes to a loop of Ravel's *Bolero*. Occasionally someone answered: a mysterious party—male? female? mythical creature?—could be heard breathing at the other end for a minute before abruptly hanging up.

Hayao Kamajii continued to elude them in space and time.

Rivière-du-Loup was already registering 25°C in early June, when I started my summer contract at the cement works.

All that remained of the sinecure of the year before was a sweet memory. In Hope's absence, I was sent to slave away in Purgatory (officially known as the bagging plant), where my job was to haul sacks of Portland cement. At the daily rate of two hundred sacks, thirty kilos per sack, I would be lugging six metric tons of cement a day, enough to pour several kilometres of Berlin Wall by the end of August.

My first day had been hell, and most of the other employees had bolted sometime earlier when I finally gathered up enough energy to stagger out of Warehouse No. 3. My legs were numb and my right shoulder was one massive bruise.

I glanced at my watch: 7:30 a.m. in Tokyo. What did that city look like at breakfast time? I pictured gutters, puddles, overcast skies—typhoon season was a few days away and they were forecasting several weeks of heavy rain. Thank you, Weather Channel.

I took a Kleenex out of my pocket and purged my sinuses of three kilos of Portland cement. It was going to be a long summer.

The Honda sputtered for a while before starting up. Its aging machinery was growing more and more fragile, and it would obviously be a few months at most before the transmission gave out, or the valves, or God knows which obscure oily organ. The best thing would be to take advantage of whatever life the car had left in it.

I headed off toward the Bunker with all the windows rolled down. My shoulder was aching and that old song about mining was playing on the radio: "Sixteen Tons." A little too close to home.

Out on the open road, I started to cry like a baby, due to the combination of the wind and the cement trapped under my eyelids. I had brought along my swimming trunks and decided to take a cold dip in the municipal swimming pool, even if, without Hope, the place would probably seem pretty grim.

Something was not right—I sensed it even before rounding the corner of the arena and catching sight of the swimming pool. There was something hovering in the air—an abnormal, suspicious smell: mouldy lumber, heating oil, crushed concrete. The area was ringed by roads department fences.

Sitting on the hood of the Honda, with a lump in my throat, I looked at the excavator reigning over a hill of planks and pipes: what was left of the municipal swimming pool locker rooms. They had demolished the fence, no doubt to clear a path for the trucks, thus partially exposing a deep crater surrounded by pieces of concrete, twisted reinforcement rods and bits of turquoise tile. Floating amid the debris was a lonely bright red lifebuoy.

I watched the excavator for a long time. It was a gigantic, shining new Mitsubishi with scarcely a few scratches showing on its paint. There was no denying, the barbarians were better equipped than in AD 546.

74. KILLING TIME

Hope opened her eyes. A ray of sunlight reached across the floor as far as her hand. She stretched a little, heard the rasp of a lighter on the other side of the futon, followed by a deep inhalation and the distinctive stench of Dubek No. 9. Merriam was smoking her first cigarette of July.

"You were talking in your sleep," Hope said.

Intrigued, Merriam propped herself up on an elbow.

"Oh, really? What was I saying?"

"No idea. What language do you dream in?"

Merriam took a puff, with an air of giving it some serious thought.

"Good question. I think I still dream in Hebrew."

"Even after four years in Japan?"

"Even after four years in Japan."

She rubbed her nose and blinked her right eye.

"I guess that should mean something . . ."

Her sentence was interrupted by a coughing jag. Hope frowned.

"How many cigarettes do you smoke a day?"

Merriam shrugged.

"Dunno. I'm trying to quit."

While Merriam carefully took another drag on her cigarette, Hope sat up with her legs crossed and grabbed a little plastic box containing a set of miniature instruments: scissors, three nail clippers in different sizes, a series of files, a pumice stone and a cuticle trimmer. She spread her tools out on the quilt and launched into an intense manicure. Since her nails were already short, she was working on a scale of a fraction of a millimetre, applying microscopic file strokes, refining a curve, meticulously shaping a cuticle.

Merriam watched her work for a moment.

"How many times a day do you cut your nails?"

"Dunno. I'm trying to quit."

Merriam doused her cigarette and shut herself in the bathroom, from which various aquatic noises could be heard. She emerged after a couple of minutes with a gloomy look on her face.

"*Attention, camarade*: We are entering menstrual no man's land."

"The what?"

"You've never heard this? When several girls live together,

their menstrual cycles eventually become synchronized. Due to pheromones, I suppose."

She began to rifle through the cupboards in search of something to eat. Hope pouted and went at her left index finger with a curved file.

"Well, you know, I've never had a period. And that certainly isn't about to change in Tokyo."

Merriam stopped searching.

"You've never had a period?"

"Never."

"Childhood disease?"

"Nah. No disease, no injury, no deformity. I'm a medical mystery."

Merriam scratched her head, taken aback by what she had just learned, or by the lack of food in the cupboards— it was hard to say which. Finally, she roused herself.

"Get up, comrade! We're going out to eat. My treat!"

It was nearly noon, and the pocket-sized snack bar was swarming with people. They sat down at the counter and the owner bellowed at them in a blend of Yiddish and Japanese. They ordered the standard smoked meat tasting of kelp, with a dubious pickle on the side, along with a serving of tempura and a large cup of oily tea.

Merriam opened her pack of cigarettes: only three left. She would soon have to restock. She always smoked more during typhoon season, a meteorological mania acquired upon arriving in Japan and which she was now unable to give up.

She lit her cigarette, blew a stream of bluish smoke toward the ceiling.

"Well, what are your plans for the day?"

"The usual. Find Hayao Kamajii. What about you?"

"The usual. Kill time."

Two plates showed up in front of them. Merriam twisted her cigarette butt into an ashtray and bit into a piece of tempura.

"I thought of something last night. How would you feel about working at the Jaffa? You have to face facts: it may be months before you find Kamajii."

Hope turned the idea over in her mind. Living in Tokyo was expensive and there were several months left before October 12, the date printed on her return ticket. She had already borrowed a fair amount from Merriam, who pushed generosity to the point of not keeping a count, but Hope knew the exact sum she owed, down to the last yen. Working at the Jaffa would allow her to pay off her debt and afford her a certain degree of freedom.

She promised to think it over.

It was two weeks since the last trace of the municipal swimming pool had been completely erased. Not one chunk of concrete remained. The roads department workers had raked the ground, unrolled a few strips of turf and installed a sign announcing the upcoming construction of a youth centre. All of a sudden, I felt old.

The demolition of a dilapidated outdoor swimming pool represented a minor change in the overall scheme of an entire city—even a city the size of Rivière-du-Loup—but to me it nevertheless seemed as if an essential part of reality had just disappeared. Without that crumbling old swimming pool, the universe felt slightly off kilter.

I felt a growing disinterest in the world above ground. When I was not busy hefting bags of cement, I stayed holed up in the Bunker. I reread the collected works of Isaac Asimov, keeping the telephone within reach—just in case, after months of radio silence, Hope Randall might deign to remember my existence and phone number.

It had just gotten dark when my mother called down to me from the top of the stairs.

"Michel? Could you go get me some things at the grocery store?"

Yawning, I grabbed the list that she held out to me: a pint of 2% milk, a loaf of sliced multigrain bread, margarine—the absurd sort of staples that you never noticed were missing before 9 p.m.

The Honda had been taken to the garage the day before and I decided to get out the old CCM that was rusting away in the depths of the shed and had not been greased or oiled for a number of summers. I inflated the tires, checked the brakes—and then, off to Steinberg's.

The supermarket was quiet and I strolled unhurriedly along the aisles. I paused for a moment at the bin of Mofuku ramen. There was the perpetual sale—3 for 99¢—and the perpetual pink and yellow astronaut. The USSR had fallen, municipal swimming pools were being eradicated, but those infuriating ramenauts were still holding on. True, our civilization was evolving, but not necessarily in the right direction.

I was leaving the supermarket when I heard sirens.

There was an orange glow in the sky on the far side of the shopping centre. It was clearly a fire, but I could not figure out what could be burning in that direction, aside from the municipal arena and a narrow vacant lot—in other words, nothing really flammable. I hopped on my bicycle, tied my bags to the handlebars and set out in the direction of the fire.

Scientific discovery of the day: Yes, a baseball stadium can burn.

I had trouble understanding how fire could spread in

an empty structure like the bleachers, but in the end maybe that old dry wood had only been waiting for the right opportunity.

The police were surveying the different entrances to the site, and a dozen firefighters were in the midst of a confab, huddled in a semicircle near the trucks. Apparently, this was their first-ever stadium fire and they were trying to decide how to approach the blaze: Would it be better to make their way across right field or over home plate, or whether (more fundamentally) it was really worth the trouble to save the creaky old wreck.

They finally uncoiled the hoses, hooked them up to a fire hydrant planted at the edge of the vacant lot and started spraying, but there was a visible lack of conviction in the operation. A column of smoke rose into the sky, black on black.

I pedalled away, neither rushing nor looking back. When I arrived home, flakes of soot were snowing down on the neighbourhood.

76. THE NINETEENTH STOP

The address of Mekiddo changed more quickly than the local weather. That day, their offices were to be found in the Gilo borough, at the other end of the city. According to Merriam, the train ride there would take an hour.

Hope took just enough money to pay the return fare, pocketed her *Rough Planet* and set out immediately. She liked to think that speed was important, that one day she would succeed in overtaking Mekiddo. Up to then, she had lost the race twenty-seven times.

Tokyo was between rush hours and the suburban trains were quiet. The passengers got on and off without saying a word, lost in thought. Housewives, toothless centenarians, miscellaneous riders.

Hope stepped off at the nineteenth stop, light years from the city centre. The streets around the station were fragrant with hibiscus and wood fires. There was something about this neighbourhood, a kind of aura, despite the nondescript architecture. Gilo had evidently been an outlying village. Tokyo had swallowed it up during the sixties, but the village spirit was still lurking in the vicinity of the train station.

Rough Planet in hand, Hope walked for about ten minutes until she reached the address she was looking for. Needless to say, however, there wasn't the slightest trace left of Mekiddo. At any rate, why would a multinational locate in a neighbourhood like this? Instead, there stood a new baseball stadium, which looked as if it had gone up the night before. The box office still smelled of fresh paint and some employees were sweeping up. A group of kids were already playing on the field.

Hope bought a can of Star Cola at a vending machine, but just as she hit the button, she realized her mistake: she had just spent the money for her return ticket!

She banged her head a few times against the vending machine. Dispirited, she nevertheless collected her beverage and climbed the bleachers to sit down.

The players were no more than twelve years old and wore Tokyo Swallows uniforms that were too big for them. The only sound was the whack of the balls and the occasional shout. The newly drawn lines were so neat as to appear unreal.

Hope looked around for an adult but saw none. She tried to imagine a world that, through some mysterious disaster, had been rid of all humans over twelve years old. The result, she mused, would not exactly be the apocalypse—more like a Charlie Brown comic strip.

Sitting in the uppermost bleachers, she could make out the tops of the downtown skyscrapers, like the echo of a distant universe. How on earth was she going to get back to the Jaffa? She searched through her pockets—on the off chance—but came up with nothing but her old train ticket, duly cancelled. She tore it into bits and scattered them on the breeze.

Shouts rose up from the playing field. A boy was trying to steal third base. He dashed away and then drifted into his slide, raising a cloud of reddish dust. The ball arrived a second too late: he was safe.

At that exact moment, the man entered the ballpark.

He wore a black suit and a tie, despite the heat, and a New York Mets cap. Hope thought he looked like a major league scout. He stationed himself behind the backstop and glanced mechanically at the game. Then he scanned the bleachers, shielding his eyes against the sun, until he spotted Hope, at which point he calmly climbed up the steps, greeted her with a nod and, gesturing, asked if he could sit down beside her.

Hope did not object.

They followed the game for a while without speaking. Hope wondered whether it was Japanese etiquette that required a person to go sit next to a stranger, and if she might find an appropriate phrase in her *Rough Planet*. She leafed through it momentarily, wavering between *You moto zai / sumi no firutaa o sagashi te i masu?* ("I'm looking for some iodine tablets / carbon filters") and *Sekijuuji no kyuukyuu sha ga tooru no o mi mashi ta ka?* ("Did you see the Red Cross ambulance go by?").

Inexpressive but courteous, never taking his eyes of the field, the man said, "*Vous pouvez me parler en français, Mademoiselle Randall.*"

"Have you heard from Hope?"

My father stepped out of the shower as I was leaving for the cement plant. He had been working late for some time and sleeping in until 7:30 a.m.

I shook my head. No, no word from Hope. He sniffed and ran his hand over his face to check his shave. One of those eloquent father-son dialogues.

Sitting on the stairs in the hallway, I was lacing up my workboots when I heard him blurt out a loud and unexpected "shit!" (My father rarely indulged in immoderate language.)

He had drawn back the curtains in the living room to look at God knows what.

I went out to see what in the outside world could be so disturbing. At first sight, nothing. I headed toward the front of the bungalow, where I saw Madame Sicotte, our neighbour three doors down, walking in the middle of the street, looking distraught, her bathrobe half-open.

"Madame Sicotte?!"

She slowly turned her head in my direction. Her face was ashen, her eyes red and the left side of her robe was streaked with blood. There was a gaping wound on her neck, a bite from a Rottweiler or something of that magnitude.

Never had I seen a gaze so vacant.

She let out a harsh groan, and I instinctively recoiled toward my house. My father was watching through the living room window, coffee cup in hand. We looked at each other incredulously. He signalled that he was going to make a call to ask for help. I asked myself who exactly he planned on calling—the police, the fire department, the army?

Madame Sicotte had swung around and was now moving toward me, dragging her feet. At that speed it would take her a while to reach me. Still, I opened the door to the Honda and put one foot inside. Just in case.

In windows nearby, curtains could be seen cautiously opening—but no one seemed in a hurry to come out and get a closer look at the situation.

A few minutes later an ambulance screeched into my field of vision. A pair of Clint Eastwoods climbed out, stethoscopes around their necks, thumbs hooked into their belts. Madame Sicotte instantly moved toward them. The two paramedics traded meaningful glances and then brought out the rubber straps.

Standing behind me, overwhelmed by the events, my father looked on. He had never seen a zombie movie—the poor guy's education was incomplete.

While the paramedics were endeavouring to immobilize Madame Sicotte on the stretcher, our old neighbour struggled, drooled, scratched, gnashed her teeth, all the time emitting that inhuman groan. They finally managed to strap her down, slid her into the ambulance and sped away.

My father looked as if he were about to have a nervous breakdown. I placed my hand on his shoulder, trying to come up with some reassuring words—but nothing came to mind. What could anyone say? Everything was unravelling since Hope had taken off.

78. THIRTY-SEVEN MINUTES

Hope felt her heart pounding all the way to her temples. To regain some composure, she took a gulp of Star Cola. Her hand trembled a little.

"You speak French?"

"The Kamajiis have a gift for foreign tongues."

A boy came up to bat and hit a home run. There was a sharp *crack* and the ball went sailing over centre field at a perfect angle.

While Kamajii's eyes followed the ball's trajectory, Hope surreptitiously looked him over. Fortyish, at most. Thin, nervous, shaggy-haired under the cap. His suit was stained, his shirt badly ironed and the knot in his necktie (a botched half-Windsor) appeared much too slack. His whole bearing suggested that he would rather have been elsewhere but that he had accepted this unpleasant task out of loyalty to the company—or some other exotic concept belonging to the Japanese econosphere.

The ball dropped well beyond the fence and three players ran off to hunt it down. Kamajii turned toward Hope with a troubled look.

"You seem disappointed to meet me."

"What bothers me is that I didn't find you first."

"That would have been most surprising. We have been watching you since you visited our offices in Seattle, in March."

"You've been following me for four months?"

"One hundred and twenty-seven days, to be exact. You have travelled an impressive distance."

"I have good boots."

Hope shielded her eyes and looked at Tokyo. The sun was beginning to set and the downtown skyscrapers seemed farther away than ever.

"You might have come to see me sooner."

"We thought you would give up your investigation after a few weeks."

"The Randalls have a stubborn streak."

"Indeed. Your obstinacy has started to be a source of concern for our company. That is why I was sent to meet you."

"In other words, you've been sacrificed."

He squinted in vague amusement.

"We would simply like to spare you a waste of energy."

Hope made a sign of acknowledgment. Reassured, Kamajii thrust his hand into his jacket and drew out a pack of Noblesse Light cigarettes. He offered one to Hope, who declined. He slipped one between his lips and looked at his watch.

"Do you think that thirty-seven minutes will be sufficient?"

79. *CROSSWORDS WEEKLY*

Thrown off balance, Hope fidgeted with her can of Star Cola. What exactly did she want to ask Kamajii? She was afraid to look foolish.

But was there anything to be gained from splitting hairs? She had crossed North America and the Pacific Ocean for the purpose of asking just one simple question, no matter how silly it might seem: Why, of all possible dates, had he chosen July 17, 2001?

Kamajii greeted the question with an approving nod.

"It was not I who chose the date, but rather the date that chose me."

"Excuse me?"

Kamajii lowered the visor of his cap. He gave the impression of following the baseball game—it was mid-inning and the two teams were trading positions—but in fact he was looking for the right words. It had been some time since he had last spoken French and he did not wish to make any errors.

"The story begins in 1971. I was twelve years old and my family had just moved. To tell the truth, we had been expropriated. Our neighbourhood had been razed in order to make room for a highway."

"You were living in Tokyo?"

"Yes. A few kilometres from here. I could show you exactly where my school was located, under an interchange . . ."

The first hitter stepped up to the plate, spat into his hands, whipped the bat around a few times.

"That summer, we lost everything. Our noodle restaurant, our house, our friends. The monetary compensation we were given was inadequate to open a new restaurant, and my father spent his days looking for work. The apartment where we lived was squalid, overcrowded and in a bad neighbourhood. I slept in the bathroom. There was a heat wave and each night I was afflicted by nightmares . . . various nightmares."

The cigarette hung from his lips. He had not yet lit it and seemed to have no intention of doing so. It quivered to the rhythm of his speech like the needle of a seismograph.

"Then, one night, I experienced . . . something different. It was not an ordinary nightmare. It was a vision."

"A vision?"

"I woke up in the middle of the apocalypse. Flames. Melting asphalt. Corpses piled one on top of the other. I will spare you the details. Actually, I have already written all this in my book."

Hope cautiously concurred. She did not dare admit that she had never read the book (which, come to think of it, was an aggravating factor in her Tokyo escapade).

The batter hit a low ball toward left field. It bounced a few times before being trapped by the shortstop, who hurled it to first base. From there, the ball flew swiftly and fluidly around the field.

"Do you know if other members of your family ever had similar visions?"

"I am not aware of that. We do not discuss these matters."

"So why did you write your book?"

The batter, called out at first, jogged back to the dugout.

"The idea came to me while I was in the airplane to Seattle. For the first time in my life I was going to find myself thousands of kilometres from my family. No one would know me. I think now that this may have been the only reason why I had applied for a position overseas . . ."

He paused momentarily while he pondered this hypothesis.

"In short, when my new supervisor suggested that I westernize my name, I jumped at the opportunity. In the telephone directory of Seattle, I chose the most ordinary identity of all. A camouflage."

"Charles Smith!"

"Precisely. There were almost sixty of them in the metropolitan area of Seattle."

There was an awkward silence. A new batter came up to the plate.

"Thus, I wrote down my vision and sent it to approximately fifteen magazines, chosen at random. I was quite unschooled in these matters. The manuscript arrived at the office of a publisher in New York."

"Sammy Levy?"

"You know him?"

"I met him. A charming man."

They exchanged a brief, knowing smile.

"At that time, Levy was publishing the *Crosswords Weekly*, a collection of puzzles and word games. He included a very abridged version of my text in the puzzle section. Readers who decoded the secret message were eligible to win a 1980 Ford Mustang."

"But there was no coded message and no Ford Mustang."
He nodded.

"The text achieved some notoriety. Readers began to make photocopies or even to copy it by hand. Homemade editions were sold in taverns and on street corners. Public readings were held. Such a success was unhoped for. Frankly, I began to feel somewhat anxious. I was losing control of the situation."

He loosened his necktie a little.

"Things deteriorated when Levy decided to publish a complete, authorized edition. I found myself with hundreds of thousands of readers. Many of them were not willing to settle for just a prophecy—they needed a piece of prophet as well. They converged on Seattle and . . ."

"And your camouflage couldn't hold up."

He sighed.

"This went on for two years. Then, fearing that the whole business would draw too much attention, my superiors repatriated me to Tokyo."

Kamajii seemed to become aware once again of the cigarette between his lips. He grabbed it, looked at it as though it had just emerged from an interdimensional gap, and put it back in its package, which he then slipped into his jacket pocket.

On the field, the baseball game had broken up into little groups, and some boys began to collect their equipment. But Kamajii had barely hit his stride. Visibly pleased to practise his French, he had launched into a tirade about the uneasy relationship that Tokyo residents maintained with the end of the world.

"You know, many of us believe the apocalypse must begin here."

Hope sipped on her now flat Star Cola.

"First time I've ever considered the end of the world from a local perspective."

"Strange, isn't it?"

"The Japanese read too many mangas."

Kamajii looked at his watch with an air of detachment.

"In fact, this is a rather ancient sentiment. Several theories exist on this subject. Some, for example, see the influence of Buddhism. Others point to the successive destructions of Tokyo—earthquakes, typhoons, bombardments. In this regard, our town planners have greatly contributed to distorting the collective psyche. Finally, there are those who believe that it is simply one facet of nationalism—the vain belief that the apocalypse must begin on Japanese soil."

His tone became reassuring.

"But, you know, not all of us share this point of view."

Kamajii vanished without any warning. He announced that he would be gone for a minute, walked down the bleachers and went into the chemical toilet that had been left behind after the stadium's construction. He never came out.

After ten minutes, Hope began to worry and went to knock on the door.

"Monsieur Kamajii?"

No answer. The toilet door opened a crack and Hope saw that there was no one inside. Yet not for an instant had she let the latrine out of her sight. The mysterious man had just evaporated—a unique ability that Mekiddo employees perhaps acquired through their repeated unexpected moves.

Hope imagined the process of his disappearance: first the feet, then the legs, the upper body, and finally the face, with the lopsided smile lingering for a few seconds in the twilight.

The sun was going down, and there was a warm wind blowing across the city. Hope consulted her *Rough Planet* and estimated that a mere 20 kilometres stood between her and the Jaffa, about three hours on foot. She decided to walk.

As she walked through the door of the Jaffa, Hope had the fleeting, reassuring impression of coming home. A dozen students were drinking beer in a corner, a cassette tape of Hebrew dub played softly, and Merriam sat at the counter, finishing a bowl of soup.

"A small dose, comrade?"

Hope accepted, and almost instantly a steaming bowl materialized under her nose. As she waited for the broth to cool down, she absentmindedly trailed her chopsticks among the freeze-dried flakes of chives. Meanwhile, Merriam drained her bowl.

"So, you're late tonight."

"I just walked from Gilo."

Whistle of admiration. Hope affected an air of modesty.

"It's just 20 kilometres."

Hope swallowed some broth, wondering whether she should mention her meeting with Hayao Kamajii. She decided against it. She had completed her Mission and there was nothing left to say.

She took off her Tony Lamas, which, toward the end of her hike, had felt uncomfortable. The left heel was starting to come loose and several seams had given out. Hope had put an inordinate amount of kilometres on the boots since arriving in Tokyo. They made hardly a sound as they dropped into the wastebasket behind the bar. Hope wiggled her toes in the air with a sense of relief.

Merriam glanced at the boots: two pieces of smoking leather.

"Can you imagine how people saw the world before the invention of the automobile?"

Hope sucked up a scalding braid of noodles. She had no specific opinion on the subject, except that, in light of her recent experience, everything must have appeared considerably farther away.

"Yes, of course. But it's more complicated than that. These days, everyone moves at roughly the same speed. Back then, it varied a lot, so, as a result, the perceived distance varied as well."

She took out her pack of No. 9 and lit herself a cigarette.

"In a region like Palestine, for example, someone on horseback could cover 65 kilometres a day. A single individual on foot, about 40. A well-disciplined army could rarely do better than 30 kilometres. And if you added a herd of goats, the distance was reduced even further."

She looked around for an ashtray and finally dropped her ashes in the sink.

"Nothing travelled more slowly than a family. If you were burdened with people who were old or lame, young children or, still worse, pregnant women, the average speed dropped below 15 kilometres a day. Under normal conditions that would not make a huge difference . . ."

Puff of cigarette.

"On the other hand, if you were fleeing from a threat—Pharaoh's army, an infestation of the living dead, or the almighty wrath of Yahweh—well, that changed everything."

Another puff.

"Doesn't that throw an interesting light on the New Testament? The story begins with a pregnant woman riding a donkey toward Bethlehem. The very picture of vulnerability. Troubled times, dangerous roads—but the woman is in no hurry. She knows things that the reader doesn't. She knows that there are still seven hundred pages to go before the Apocalypse."

She doused her cigarette in the sink.

"Impressive, don't you think?"

Hope sat there without speaking or moving, but only stared into empty space holding her chopsticks in mid-air.

"*Hé, camarade, ça va?*"

Hope roused herself and seemed to come back down to earth. Merriam poured her a large glass of mineral water, adding three sections of lemon.

"You're dehydrated. What an idea, walking 20 kilometres in the middle of a heat wave! Here, drink this."

Hope shook her head.

"No, I'm okay. I was just thinking of something. Old memories."

Merriam's frown was both menacing and maternal, and Hope meekly drained her mineral water. Satisfied, Merriam wiped down the steel countertop, unfolded her copy of *Ha'aretz* and went to work on the daily crossword.

Hope finished her noodles without saying another word and slipped away via the secret stairway. Once on the roof, she took a long look at Tokyo burning—tens of thousands of light bulbs, neon lights, fluorescents, sodium lampposts. Billions of kilolemons per second.

At last she felt safe.

83. UNDER A DIFFERENT LIGHT

August 1989. Route 185 was baking under a Sinai sun. Behind the spruce trees, an army of peat harvesters raised a cumulonimbus of reddish dust that was visible for kilometres in every direction.

On the shoulder of the road sat Ann Randall's deceased Lada, hood half-raised, all windows down. An uninterrupted stream of traffic brushed past the carcass without even slowing down: Winnebagos, top-heavy cars, aluminum rowboats perched on trailers. A whole nation of vacationers returning from the Atlantic provinces, totally satiated, totally unaware that the end of the world was due to take place any day.

While her mother discussed transmissions and carbure-tors with the tow-truck driver, Hope paced up and down next to the car. She kicked the door and, leaning on the roof, eyed the inside of the vehicle with a look of annoyance.

Now, in the middle of the day, she saw the interior in a different light.

She looked at the seats overflowing with bags, clothes, provisions, canned goods, the bottles of ketchup and relish stacked on the floor, the jars of pickles, the bags of salt and flour, the rubber boots, the umbrella wedged under the handbrake, the two enormous bags of rice piled on the front passenger seat, the tuque and gloves, the heaps of ramen packages, the bibles, the twelve dust masks and three flashlights.

And amid the chaos, in the corner of the back seat, Hope's minuscule space—barely enough room for a young girl.

A young girl, or an extra case of ramen.

84. A THREE-THOUSAND-YEAR VOYAGE

The moon was rising over Rivière-du-Loup. A freight train trundled by on the other side of the street—two tiers of assorted containers: Maersk, Hapag-Lloyd, Hanjin and China Shipping. The usual parade. The loco-motive was already far down the track, and one could hear the screeching of the rails and the occasional whistle of a poorly sealed compressed-air duct.

It was dead calm at the Ophir. A Dalai Lama was dozing at the counter with his nose in a bowl of pretzels, under the maternal eye of Ann Randall. In a corner—surprise!—the TV was tuned to BBC with the volume turned down. I imagined Hope nestled in the shadows, holding the remote control.

"Hey there, Mickey! Long time no see!"

I half waved and installed myself at the counter. My work clothes were shedding particles of cement. Ann Randall, who had obviously read my mind, set down a frosty mug of pale ale in front of me.

"It's on the house, honey!"

I raised my glass to her health and took a gulp. Countless alcohol molecules instantly exploded in my brain, a thousand magnesium flashbulbs going off together. Dozens of tiny knots loosened at the core of my tender muscles. Proletarian drinking habits suddenly appeared to make sense.

We talked for a while. A scattered exchange without any specific goal: It's been a while, the bar's pretty quiet, how about this heat wave, they say it's hard on the farmers.

From time to time, I glanced distractedly at the screen. There were shots of an Israeli military airport, where the airlift of fifteen thousand Ethiopian Jews was being completed—an exploit that had required only thirty-odd airplanes.

"These people," an Israeli journalist exclaimed, "are ending a three-thousand-year voyage."

The muted whine of the dishwasher could be heard, or perhaps it was the snoring of a Dalai Lama—the distinction was not easy to make. I took another swig of beer. "Do you want to watch something else?" Ann Randall asked, offering me the remote control. I declined.

Standing in front of a jet engine nozzle, the BBC reporter talked about the climate of instability in the Somali Peninsula, repeated that Israel had just smashed a number of records with this exceptional resettlement. The servicemen had even removed the seats from some of the 747s in order to squeeze in more passengers. The journalist noted in conclusion that several women had apparently given birth during the flight.

I whistled. To be born in an overcrowded Boeing— now there was an omen of an exceptional future, right? Ann Randall smiled politely—she had not really been listening.

The report ended with images of refugees kissing the tarmac. This was followed by an update from Iraq, and I turned my attention away from the screen. Ann Randall was pouring herself a small cognac.

"Have you heard any news from Hope?"

She gave me an inquiring look and put the bottle back without corking it.

"Me? No. Why do you ask?"

I toyed with my beer mug, somewhat nervous, after all, about venturing onto such private territory. Ann had evidently not even noticed that Hope had left town.

"Left? Where?"

"Japan."

She raised her eyebrows, as if to say "well that would explain a lot of things," and took another sip of cognac.

"How long ago?"

"Four months. Five, pretty soon. I thought you knew. She hasn't called you?"

"No."

On the TV screen, Hans Blix was commenting on the UN inspections in Iraq. Saddam Hussein had agreed to abandon his weapons of mass destruction, to suspend his chemical, biological and nuclear arms programs, to destroy his long-range missiles and to no longer allow children to play with penknives and matches. The West had nothing more to worry about.

A minute went by in almost total silence. Each of us drank without saying anything. The Dalai Lama turned over onto his left side. A few pretzel crumbs fell from his hair.

I didn't dare ask the questions that were nagging me: Why had Hope gone away? Why the radio silence? Only a Randall could have answered those questions, but I doubted that Ann would be able to recall what was going on inside her own head the night she decamped from Yarmouth, nearly leaving her daughter behind.

Rather than putting the questions to her directly, I announced that Hope had found her date.

"Which date?"

"The date of the end of the world."

"Oh?"

There was an awkward silence. Maybe I hadn't been specific enough.

"According to her, it will happen on July 17, 2001."

Ann Randall appeared to be analyzing this new data, like a teacher evaluating her student's work.

"Good date," she finally declared. "Prime numbers, Mickey, that's the secret."

She poured herself a finger of cognac and said nothing more.

Damned Randalls.

After a while I got tired of hearing about Saddam Hussein. I drained my beer and went out for a walk.

In the moonlight, the city looked like a Japanese water-colour, and the paper mill emitted an odour of rotten eggs. I ended up at the municipal stadium or, to be exact, at the place where the municipal stadium had stood a few weeks earlier.

Not even the slightest evidence was left of the fire. The day after, the rubble had been removed and the ground levelled by a bulldozer. The municipal council had voted in favour of rebuilding a larger, better-equipped stadium on the outskirts of the city. The layout of two new streets and the construction of thirty condominium units were announced a week later, and an illustrated sign was put up at the perimeter of the site, like a giant postcard from Eden. I was surprised at how quickly the project had been set in motion. Someone somewhere seemed to be in a hurry to obliterate whatever was left of the old stadium, to erase it from collective memory. It seemed almost suspicious.

The sign resembled a modernist manifesto. Boundless optimism, perfectly trimmed hedges. You could sense the echoes of the postwar boom. The only things missing were plutonium-fuelled cars, household robots and velocopters.

Standing beside me, Hope examined the billboard with a sarcastic smile.

"Yessir, it sure looks clean and tidy."

She turned away from the billboard toward the adjacent streets. Etched against the moonlight were the bluish silhouettes of the bungalows, perforated here and there by TV screens.

"Can you imagine what the world looked like before?"

"Before what?"

"Before bungalows."

I frowned. Yes, I knew what the world looked like before. I had seen archival photos at an exhibition of the historical society. This poorly drained depression was once an ancient peat bog. Spruce, reddish lakes covered with sphagnum. Flowering pitcher plants, water lilies, probably a few migrating birds' nests. Frogs, bulrushes, mosquitoes, flies, butterflies, dragonflies. Muskrats, raccoons, garter snakes. Countless small animals, bacteria, single-celled organisms.

The results of millions of years of evolution.

Hope sighed.

"Can you imagine the effort it takes to *wipe out* a peat bog? It doesn't happen on its own. You have to drain the land, unload thousands of tons of gravel, level the ground with bulldozers, graders, steamrollers. Dig sewers, plan streets. Install water and electricity systems."

All at once, my view of the surrounding bungalows shifted: Now they encircled the empty lot and were preparing to close in on it and bury it in silence—like a blanket of peat moss on the surface of a lake. One world swallowing another.

"The UN inspectors can say what they like, the fact remains that the bungalow is the primary weapon of mass destruction invented during the Cold War."

I burst out laughing. Who but Hope could be so matter-of-fact in spouting such fantastically outrageous comments?

The laughter stuck in my throat. I suddenly, brutally, realized the magnitude of my mistake. Like an idiot, I had let Hope run off to the far side of the world without reacting, instead of going after her to convince her to turn around or disappear along with her. But I had done nothing. Now it was too late, and I knew she would not be coming back.

Alone on a vacant lot, I watched the world disintegrate around me.

86. DOES ANYONE STILL TALK
ABOUT NUCLEAR WINTER?

I grew up in a world obsessed by the apocalypse.

On the playground of my primary school, the atomic holocaust was just another topic of discussion. Between games of hopscotch we would talk about bunkers, radiation, plutonium and megatons. Some of us, though completely hopeless in mathematics, could cite detailed statistics on the Soviet nuclear arsenal, and this quantified knowledge made our fears all the more tangible. Who would get their share of Soviet warheads? Would we die roasted, vaporized or irradiated?

We were the pre-war generation.

Bunkers were only halfway reassuring. Who would want to spend three weeks crammed together below ground, eating sardines packed in oil, playing poker with matches and defecating into a tin can, only to resurface at the dawn of a nuclear winter that was going to last forty more years?

We were a little taken aback by the fall of the USSR. No matter—there was still acid rain, the disappearing ozone layer, carcinogenic substances, cholesterol, desertification, the fluoridation of drinking water, asteroids, whatever. The specifics didn't matter, so long as it was imminent.

We saw the end of the world everywhere. As far as we

were concerned, even a trivial change of date was liable to trigger the collapse of civilization or at least a return to the Middle Ages and everything that that entailed: black plague, cholera, carnage, crusades . . . elevator breakdowns. The Gregorian calendar as a catalyst for destruction—why hadn't someone thought of that before?

On the night of December 31, 1999, the dials slowed down in one time zone after another—but nothing happened, and the sun rose over a civilization unscathed. True, a grandmother in the suburbs of Pittsburgh lost her weekly shopping list, but everywhere else human beings continued to get high, to copulate and to keep an eye on the stock markets. Kids still combed through the garbage in the dumps of Calcutta. Other kids, in Sierra Leone, polished their old Yugoslavian AK-47s. Thousands of pumps sucked out oil through the Earth's crust. Why should anyone have been concerned about the end of the world?

Greenhouse gases, tsunamis, particle accelerators, radon, nanotechnologies, the market economy, black holes, epidemics of neuro-eruptive infants, peak oil, ice-nine, the reorientation of the Earth's axis and deorbiting episodes, genetic mutations, azoospermia, the atrophy or hypertrophy of the Sun, sticky or scaly creatures emerging from the ocean depths, the inversion of the poles, the industrial transformation of human beings into chipboard panels, increasing entropy, gravitational anomalies, androids, pelagic methane, saturated fat and hydrogenated fat, bird flu pandemics, pesticides and/or herbicides, riots, antibiotics and the People's Republic of China. The list of perils looked more and more like the ingredients printed on a package of ramen—an implausible inventory. But we had gone beyond the point of any plausibility. We had been expecting the end of the world for so long that it was now part of our DNA.

Anyway.

I often thought about all this. Not every night, but almost. I may even have been thinking about it at the exact moment Ann Randall died at the age of forty-seven years and four months. The death certificate was signed at the Hôtel-Dieu, the hospital of Rivière-du-Loup, just before midnight on July 13, 2001.

"A very bad date," Hope would have declared.

87. INCANDESCENT WAVES

The news of Ann Randall's death reached me at noon. All my co-workers had gone out to eat, leaving me in conversation with my computer. I didn't really feel like going outdoors: for several days Montreal had sat under a layer of yellowish air, and just looking through the window was enough to make me choke. I was eating a repulsive tuna sandwich while reading the forecasts on Environment Canada's website (smog warning in effect) when my father's message showed up on my screen.

From: J. Bauermann

Date: 15 July 2001 12:16:45 EST

Subject: Re: RE: Re:

Ann randall pass ed on two days ago. Stroke or r uptured

aneurysm. No view ing, wake a t the ophir tonight.

Paternal restraint in all its splendour.

I read the message three times, unsure of exactly what my feelings were. I wavered between tears and laughter. How could Ann Randall have dared to die four days before the end of the world? At this level, irony surely had to be renamed.

I closed the message and went back to the weather forecasts. The map of warm fronts painted all of Ontario in incandescent waves. It didn't bode well for us.

I flipped through my datebook. Nothing very urgent planned for the next forty-eight hours. I dropped my sandwich in the wastebasket and left a message on my supervisor's voice mail ("feeling sick, could be stomach flu, taking the rest of the day off") and decamped without even shutting down my computer.

After collecting a few personal items at my apartment—toothbrush, clothes, water bottle—I fled the island aboard my old Toyota.

88. A SERIOUS DENT IN REALITY

So, there I was, on yet another never-ending trip to my hometown: five hours of rectilinear highway, several litres of iced tea, and a break for bladder relief at the halfway point. The speakers blared out Moby in a loop—it was the only cassette in the car that was still playable. I counted the road signs, trying not to think too much.

It was late afternoon when I arrived in Rivière-du-Loup.

Some thirty cars were parked haphazardly in front of the Ophir. A few old men were conversing by the door, hands in their pockets, cigarettes in their mouths. I had an urge to turn around, but I finally parked the Toyota at the far end of the train station, near the farm co-op, and trudged over to the Ophir, still trying not to think too much. That was the main thing: not to think too much.

The wake had just begun, but the place was already packed, the air thick with sweat and smoke. They must have jettisoned the chairs, because everyone was standing.

My heart clenched, or maybe it was my stomach. What had I come here for? To pay my respects to Ann Randall, of course—but I had never been very big on funerals and I could just as well have sent a message from Montreal. Tele-condolences. Anyway, there was not one familiar face among this gloomy crowd. No hands to shake, no one to embrace. All around, regular customers were speaking in hushed voices. A few Dalai Lamas (still sober) huddled together at the counter with grim faces. Ann Randall's departure had clearly put a serious dent in reality.

I looked around for the guest of honour and spotted her on a shelf behind the bar, reduced to a few cubic centimetres of fine ash. A shovelful of Pompeii in a granite urn. A photo of Ann in her better days had been placed nearby, along with a pack of cigarillos and a bottle of Rémy Martin Grande Champagne Cognac, obviously purchased at great cost for the occasion. A generous snifter had been filled and set down for the deceased.

I found these offerings unexpectedly moving, and averted my eyes.

Robert cut through the crowd to shake my hand, as though we were old friends, which was odd since I was barely seventeen the last time we had seen each other. The prodigal son syndrome. Robert had put on weight, lost some hair. He explained how he had organized everything: the incineration, the obituary, the wake. The Ophir had in a way been Ann's home. So, had I heard anything from Hope? No. Nothing. Robert shook his head.

"You don't just abandon your mother like that, right?"

I nodded politely, but, frankly, I doubted that life was that simple.

In the absence of any close relatives, Robert had taken care of the Final Clean-up at the Pet Shop. Otherwise (he said indignantly) the owner would have dumped everything in the garbage. I wouldn't have blamed him. As I recalled, the place had already gone a long way toward dumpification. Robert admitted that he had not found much worth keeping. He had sent 20 kilos of non-perishable goods to the Saint Vincent de Paul and stuffed almost forty bags into the Chinese Garden's garbage container. The rest fit into a few boxes, one of which, by the way, was meant for me.

From under the counter, he pulled out a heavy cardboard Premium Florida Lemons crate. Under the tired flaps I discovered Ann Randall's famous collection of bibles, smelling of musk and fungus. Robert made a vaguely explanatory gesture.

"I figured this would interest you . . ."

I nodded without saying anything. After exchanging a long handshake with Robert, I left the Ophir loaded down with my box of bibles, which weighed a ton. The box went into the Toyota's trunk between my toolbox and a spare tire.

The kitchen smelled like home: tomato soup and grilled chicken. The TV was tuned to the news. My mother gave me a casual kiss, as if I'd been living in the bungalow next door (she lived outside of time and space, like all mothers).

"Have you eaten? I'll heat up some chicken for you."

My father shook my hand, asked me how the drive down had been, offered me a beer. It was strange to see him at home so early in the evening. He had sold the cement works six months before and now belonged to that population of free, unfettered men who ate dinner at a decent hour of the evening.

The sale had concluded the final chapter of the Bauermann dynasty. The concrete plant and the fleet of trucks had fallen to the enemy two years earlier. My father could have dug his heels in for another ten years, but what good would it have done, since his sons had no intention of taking over the business? The elder son was a psychoanalyst in Toronto, and the younger cultivated his scoliosis hunched in front of a monitor in a cubicle in downtown Montreal. So my father had accepted the offer of PanAmerican Concrete, a multinational that we'd heard him rail against thousands of times. After several proudly independent decades, Bauermann Concrete Inc. had finally been engulfed by the global economy. Another unwritten page in the history of the middle class, etc., etc.

My father would never admit it, but getting rid of the company had ultimately been something of a liberation. He was like Butch Cassidy: too sensitive to work in concrete.

We drank our beer as we watched TV without paying much attention. Satellite pictures of a hurricane flashed by on the screen, followed by George W. Bush standing among the rubble of a Dallas suburb. My mother placed a steaming plate in front of me.

"How's Karen?"

I set to work on the chicken while carefully calibrating my answer. "Karen has left," I finally announced as I speared a potato.

"Left? Where has she gone?"

"Nowhere. Somewhere else. She's left me. We're not together any more. Could I have the salt, please?"

A deep sense of relief washed over me. The worst was behind me. The words had been uttered, the heresy confessed.

Though my father had given up on the continuation of the business, my mother still had expectations for the continuation of the family. My brother being unofficially gay, the burden of perpetuation rested on my shoulders. My mother monitored my love life with a microscope, and each of my breakups affected her more than me. Among all the women I had been with, Karen had seemed the ideal candidate. For the first time, one of my partners fiercely wanted to have babies. Several. Soon. In fact, that was what had led to our breakup: she had grown tired of waiting for me to be ready. She had packed her bags one Thursday morning, stating that she didn't intend, quote, to procreate at forty-one like a fucking boomer.

She had taken the futon and the coffee maker.

When she heard the news, my mother shook her head. I knew what was coming. How many girlfriends had I had over the past ten years? Seven, eight? What was I thinking? I would be thirty soon and it was about time I grew up . . .

My father cut short her lecture.

"Leave him alone. He'll find someone when he's ready."

My mother sighed before backing off. My father winked at me, but it was plain to see that he too was a little concerned about my future.

90. KILN

Up at dawn, as rumpled as an old Cracker Jack wrapper, I ate breakfast with my father. He could not get used to his new role as a free man and persisted in waking up every morning at five. As for my mother, she always slept until eight. I claimed that I could not wait until then—which was, in a way, absolutely true—and promised to come for a longer visit at Thanksgiving.

My father walked me to the Toyota, barefoot, holding his coffee. He said nothing in particular to encourage me, but his Paul Newman smile did the job. Robust handshake, slap on the back—and I was off.

I was about to head toward the highway when I had a stroke of inspiration and veered off toward the industrial park.

The PanAmerican Concrete logo dominated the entrance to the cement works. A foreign body. I passed the guardhouse (unoccupied) and drove on until I was under the kiln, where the ever-present tires, plastic waste and piles of anthracite were heaped up. I opened the trunk of the Toyota, grabbed the box of bibles and dumped it among the old tires. Ten kilos of additional fuel, courtesy of Ann Randall.

After a quick stop to fill up on gas and caffeine, I was back on the 20. I put on the Moby cassette with the volume all the way up, but after hearing the first few bars I felt nauseous. I punched the Eject button and pitched the tape out the window.

I drove back to Montreal in total silence, except for the radio antenna whistling in the wind. Five hours straight, not even the briefest of pit stops. I crossed the Victoria Bridge in the early afternoon. Already, a traffic jam was forming on the west side.

I could have stayed away for the rest of the day, but a nebulous feeling nudged me in the direction of the office. Professionalism, curiosity, docility—or simply the fear of being alone with myself in the middle of the day?

As I walked through the glass doors, it occurred to me that the air conditioning alone justified the sacrifice.

As soon as I sat down at my computer I checked my email. Nothing interesting. Three Nigerian heirs were offering me a sizable commission on some colossal inheritances. I disintegrated them with my index finger—shazam!—and quickly browsed through the news. New phase of the recession in Japan. Meeting of the Arab League to counter the violence in the Middle East. Organic meat, flavour of the month.

Then I opened Google and keyed in a search for "Hope + Randall": the 345,702 results sent me reeling.

It appeared there were about fifty Hope Randalls on the planet, including a real estate agent, a Triple-A Midget hockey player, a Carmelite renamed Mary Rose of Jerusalem (1842–1903), a post-doctoral researcher in nuclear physics and an orthophonist specialized in glossalia. There were also a certain number of Randall Hopes, in particular an Olympic wrestler, a Jesuit with a degree in Danish literature and a trucker who collected tutus.

I sifted through the results, in vain. After twenty minutes, I took a different tack. I found the telephone number of the Canadian embassy in Japan and logged on to the nearest atomic clock. In the Tokyo time zone, poetically baptized +0900 UTC, it was nearly two in the morning. Most human beings there (including the Canadian diplomatic corps) were softly snoring on futons as thin as soda crackers.

A disturbing detail: as Tokyo was located to the west of the International Date Line, the local calendar already indicated July 17, 2001. The countdown had just begun, and there were only about thirty hours of anxiety left to endure.

Assuming that Tokyo had meanwhile not been wiped off the face of the earth, the embassy offices would open at around 7 p.m. Montreal time. I wrote down the telephone number, taking care not to omit any of the fourteen digits.

92. MADAME HIKARI

A typical day at work—nothing worth mentioning. On the way home I stopped at Ngô's, the local convenience store, where old Ngô himself was sitting behind the counter, laboriously filling in sudoku grids.

I bought a dozen shrimp rolls—one of Mrs. Ngô's

culinary masterpieces—a ripe-to-perfection mango, three limes and a six-pack of Heineken. As I was paying, I noticed a series of Aloha prepaid telephone cards pinned up behind the cash. The list of rates covered every country on earth, including a few dubious states not even recognized by the UN. The rate for Japan was ten cents a minute.

"Do these cards work okay?"

Mr. Ngô replied with a gently enthusiastic nod, and I added a twenty-dollar card to my bill.

When I got home, I put the rolls in the oven and the beer in the fridge. Then I picked up the telephone and dialed the twelve digits on the card followed by the fourteen digits of the Canadian embassy in Tokyo. I succeeded in getting the numbers right—a good beginning.

The embassy receptionist had trouble understanding what I was after and shunted me on to hold. Japanese-style music, faint electronic fizz. The Aloha card was doing its job, despite the slight distortions. At ten cents a minute, a degree of tolerance was in order.

My call was finally transferred to a certain Mrs. Hikari, whose French was passable. I explained my problem: I was trying to get in touch with a Canadian citizen who had been living in Japan for a number of years and whose mother had just died. Could the embassy help me find her?

Mrs. Hikari listened to me without speaking, promised to do whatever was possible (God knows what that might mean in diplomatic parlance) and took down my contact numbers at home and at work. Before hanging up she offered me her very sincere condolences.

I ate my shrimp rolls on the rear balcony with my feet up on the guardrail, inhaling long gulps of ice-cold beer. The breeze was heavy with the fragrance of flowers—the neighbour's balcony was crammed with dozens of flower boxes and pots. A genuine Buddhist sanctuary.

It was a while since the sun had gone down amid the smog, but an orange glow lingered on the horizon—an enormous blaze consuming the entire western part of Montreal.

93. AN ORDINARY DAY

Five hours of sleep, lukewarm shower, glass of juice, and away I went to punch in like a model citizen.

The scene at the Rosemont Metro station looked like something straight out of the Blitz: hundreds of travellers crowded the platform, some of them sitting on the ground. The ticket attendant explained to me that half of the underground network would be out of service for an indefinite (and, therefore, considerable) length of time.

Three separate incidents were to blame: a suicide at the Berri station, a fire in the electrical system at Lucien-L'Allier and a gas alert at Jarry.

Up to that point, July 17, 2001, had looked like an ordinary day.

I went back upstairs to take the emergency shuttle, but the situation was hardly better on the street. Two or three hundred people were waiting on the sidewalk. The usual lineup had melted down to an aggressive mass, and each time a bus stopped in front of the station, the crowd rushed the doors as if a humanitarian evacuation was under way. An ambulance was parked on the median next to someone who had been trampled or crushed against the doors, no one really knew.

I resigned myself to the pedestrian alternative. The walk downtown would take forty-five minutes, but that seemed more reasonable than risking one's life to take the bus.

When I arrived at the office, it smelled of strong coffee and panic. A California multinational had just launched a vicious takeover bid on our company, and all the signs suggested that this torpedo would reach us shortly after the financial markets opened. The future: uncertain.

I was strangely immune to the ambient anxiety. I floated outside my body, a few metres above the scene.

Midmorning, our department head called a meeting. The buyout was indeed going ahead, but it was essential to stay calm: the buyers had promised that no jobs would be cut. For the time being we would have to crank up our output because the transition required that we finish up a number of projects.

In other words, we had seventy-two hours to do several weeks of work.

The situation was crystal clear: they planned to make us sweat before announcing the layoffs. The Romans had already used this sort of method in the galleys. Around the room, my colleagues talked timetables, schedules, achievability, priorities and unpaid overtime. The union representative was on his cellphone, and the department head was slinking toward the exit.

Still hovering a few metres above myself, I observed the Styrofoam cups in which the coffee was growing cold and thinking that those damned containers would not decompose for another three thousand years. One hell of a lot of timetables.

94. TAKE HEART!

The rest of the day continued along the same lines: a power outage, two computer system crashes and a twenty-minute evacuation due to a (false) fire alarm. Emails were going around, spreading rumours of sabotage. Inevitably, the backlog built up and some of us had to be sacrificed for the common good. Single, no children—I had all the prerequisites to qualify for overtime work.

The usual quitting time had long passed when my telephone rang. A double tone, signalling an outside call. The call display said *undisclosed number*. I immediately recognized Mrs. Hikari's voice, proof positive that on the morning of July 18, 2001, Tokyo had not been swallowed up. Take heart!

But the good news stopped there.

With unsettling candour, Mrs. Hikari told me that the options for locating a Canadian citizen were quite limited. As a rule, it amounted to consulting the embassy's database (a two-minute procedure). If this produced no results, they simply gave up.

Hope was not registered in their database, but, in light of the circumstances, Mrs. Hikari had taken the liberty of giving the Japanese immigration agency a call. There was no sign of Hope there either, which meant that she had no visa and no visitor's permit.

To sum up, Mrs. Hikari explained, this left only three possibilities:

1. Hope had a tourist visa that she renewed every ninety days by leaving and then re-entering Japan (an option both onerous and costly).

2. Hope lived in Japan illegally.

3. Hope had simply left Japan.

Of course, none of these three hypotheses fell within the embassy's jurisdiction.

I could always post a small advertisement in a daily newspaper, but without harbouring any illusions: Tokyo's population was in the vicinity of thirty-six million. In order to get results, I would likely have to repeat the operation in several periodicals over a number of weeks, if not months. Mrs. Hikari offered to send me a list of addresses if I wished.

No, I did not wish.

In fact, I felt as though I did not wish anything any more.

I thanked Mrs. Hikari and hung up. The clock on my computer showed 7:14 p.m. I glanced over the partitions of the cubicles. No one in sight.

95. ETHNOLOGICAL OBSERVATION NO. 743

The human race had invented an antidote to this sort of day: Mrs. Ngô's shrimp rolls.

Out of luck: the store was closed. "Back in 5 minutes" the makeshift sign said, but even though I had a whole lifetime (or what was left of it) ahead of me, I went across the street to the MaxiPrix. Not a great place to be vaporized, but no worse, when you thought about it, than in front of a Vietnamese convenience store.

In the pharmacy, the air conditioners were set to full blast. Standing behind the cosmetics counter, a saleslady in a smock was holding a spray bottle and polishing the glass with as much enthusiasm as a clerk at the city morgue.

I headed for Aisle 5—cleaning products and food.

The ramen display was utterly mind-boggling. MaxiPrix stocked every flavour in the universe! It had been years since my last bowl of ramen—my last year of university, no doubt—and I looked around for Captain Mofuku. Not that I really had a craving—far from it—but I somehow felt nostalgic. Maybe it was just the desire to give the whole story a kind of closure with a familiar taste.

I searched all through the ramenopedia but there was no Mofuku to be found there. The company must have been absorbed by another instant-food Cyclops based in Asia.

All this rot-proof food made me lose my appetite and I quickly moved away from Aisle 5.

I strolled around the pharmacy looking for an omen and ended up in the sanitary napkins section. What sort of omen could this be?

Ethnological observation No. 743: MaxiPrix sold almost as many varieties of sanitary napkins as of ramen.

Super-absorbent, extra-thin, super-mini, long with wings, 3-D system, overnight Protection-Plus, patented solution, assured freedom. I discreetly peeled open the lid of a box. Inside, each napkin was individually wrapped in a plastic sleeve. I pictured these delicate rose petals at the bottom of the municipal dump, cheek by jowl with the Styrofoam coffee cups.

I carefully inspected the box for an expiry date. There was none.

I left the MaxiPrix empty handed. Across the street, the convenience store still announced that it would be opening in five minutes. What if the sign had been hung up two hours earlier and old Ngô had accidentally shut himself inside the beer refrigerator? I would have to face the end of the world without Mrs. Ngô's shrimp rolls. There was no end of nuisances that I would have to bear.

On the corner of the street an old orange Datsun had just overheated. The driver had lifted the hood and a plume of black smoke drifted skyward. A big Italian man burst out of the nearby jewellery store armed with a fire extinguisher, and he blanketed everything—the Datsun, the fire and the driver—in a cumulus of carbonic snow.

What sort of comedy had I stumbled into?

Back home, the mailbox had come under assault: a bagful of circulars, three bills, an offer for a credit card and the menu of a sushi bar. I climbed the stairs slowly.

My head was spinning and I urgently needed to find something edible within the next five minutes. The sushi option suddenly looked a little more attractive.

I flung down the pile of mail, which fanned out on the dining table, and I noticed a light blue envelope with a red border. Airmail paper.

A dozen Japanese stamps covered half of the envelope.

96. TODAY'S ACTIVE YOUNG JAPANESE WOMAN

I went to sit on the balcony holding the letter in one hand, a Heineken in the other, and my penknife between my teeth.

Sipping my beer several times, I looked at the envelope. I was reluctant to open or even touch this supernatural, blinding apparition. I almost expected it to disappear at any moment. But it stayed there, in my lap, unmistakably tangible.

On the reverse side someone had written an interminable address. A Tokyo address.

I imagined Hope giving the flap a lick, wiping away a pearl of saliva with her thumb and then, as serious as a child, doing a series of unbelievable quantum calculations with the stub of a pencil to make sure that the envelope would leave at the right time, cross the entire planet, going from one plane to another, from one post office to another, and arrive in my hands exactly today, at sunset.

The stamps were exquisite, a veritable trove of Japanese iconography: giant squid, Mount Fuji and several Hello Kittys.

What was I afraid of?

I finished my beer and gathered my courage. A stroke of the knife and the envelope was slit open. There was nothing in it except for a bland plastic wrapper, empty as well. Nothing else. Not a word, not a letter, not even a haiku on a Post-it.

Just an empty wrapper.

I smoothed it out with the palm of my hand and examined it carefully, intrigued at first, then incredulous, and finally a hair's breadth away from a nervous breakdown. Despite the absence of any Latin script, there could be no ambiguity as to the product that this wrapper had contained.

Sanitary napkins.

More specifically (based on my recently acquired expertise), these were extra-thin, hypoallergenic napkins with NanoNikki™ micropores and super-leakproof-yet-ultrasoft wings. A model made for today's active young Japanese woman.

Hope Randall was no longer a medical mystery.

Mirabel Airport was gently sliding downhill. Its impending death had been announced for years. Decried, despised and soon decommissioned: the great cycle of life.

As for me, I was quite happy to depart from Mirabel. Given the growing rumours of closure, I felt like a visitor among virtual ruins—the ideal blend of archaeology and science fiction. Shielded by the glass wall, I tried to imagine an abandoned airport. How much time would it take before the couch grass crept into the joints of this flawless concrete? Before the tarmac was breached by tufts of straw, by willows and dogwoods and alders?

The perennial questions of a Bauermann.

I turned away from the glass wall. The terminal was deserted, peaceful and depressing at the same time. All that was missing was a scattering of the living dead.

A few dozen passengers bided their time near Gate 12: globetrotting women on a budget, farm machinery salesmen, nuns, middle-class Mexicans drinking bottled water, migrant workers, thirty-year-olds in worn-out jeans. The grandeur and misery of the low season.

The flight attendants took their positions at the check-in counter, and I drew a whole collection of boarding passes out of my pocket. I had purchased an exotic ticket on the Internet, an unbeatable deal, which would mean flying to Acapulco, San Diego and Honolulu before finally heading for Tokyo—in total, thirty-one hours of travelling.

The time needed to think about what came next.

Behind the counter a flight attendant picked up the intercom handset, cleared her throat and welcomed us aboard Air Transat flight 1707 to Acapulco.

"This is a pre-boarding announcement. Passengers requiring assistance or travelling with small children, please proceed to Gate 12."

The passengers stood up. Stretched. Checked their luggage. A line soon formed in front of the counter. The atmosphere gradually became charged with the tension generated by the imminent departure, but I remained serene. Leaning my back against the glass wall, I fanned myself with the sheaf of boarding tickets. I felt light, immortal. I was Paul Newman.

Things were much better now that the end of the world was behind us.

ACKNOWLEDGMENTS

Despite impressions to the contrary, a novelist is never completely alone.

I wish to thank a number of people who have contributed to the making of this book, starting with Antoine Tanguay, who patiently listened to me construct and deconstruct the project, and whose maverick erudition nourished my thinking at various times. Bernard Wright-Laflamme, Martin Beaulieu and Pierre Blais read and commented on the text and corrected certain factual mistakes. Jeremy Barnes assisted me in clarifying the relationship between nuclear explosions and citrus fruits (although the calculations in Chapter 17 are my own, and I take full responsibility for the errors or inconsistencies that may be found there). Masumi Kaneko and Julie Sirois translated the *Rough Planet* excerpts. Isabel Flores Oliva was there.

A warm word of appreciation for Lazer Lederhendler, my trusted translator, who worked at a breakneck pace and produced an exceptional translation. Very special thanks go to Pamela Murray, whose enthusiasm, intelligence, and sharp eye helped make this English version into an edition in its own right. Thanks also to Shaun Oakey and Kathryn Exner. Editors exist to show that a text can still be improved after five hundred readings.

Finally, I want to express my gratitude to my family, in particular Marie Wright-Laflamme, Jean-Luc Laflamme and Louise Plante, without whose support the manuscript would have advanced at the painful rate of fifteen kilometres a day.

A NOTE ABOUT THE TYPE

Apocalypse for Beginners has been set in Janson, a misnamed typeface designed in or about 1690 by Nicholas Kis, a Hungarian in Amsterdam. In 1919 the original matrices became the property of the Stempel Foundry in Frankfurt, Germany. Janson is an old-style book face of excellent clarity and sharpness, featuring concave and splayed serifs, and a marked contrast between thick and thin strokes.

BOOK DESIGN BY CS RICHARDSON